8

▶**CHAPTER 1**
"CATASTROPHE"

▶**CHAPTER 2**
SMALL ASSASSIN

52

D0188068

CONTENTS

1

PROLOGUE

ADVENTURER, YOU WHOSE WEIGHT IS BORNE BY YOUR WINGED SOUL!

THE MYSTICAL WORLD OF THELDESIA IS HOME TO DRAGONS AND GIANTS, MAGICAL BEASTS AND DEMIHUMANS.

No one in this other world has made it all the way

from Akiba to Susukino before.

— We're the first ones who've ever seen this view.

 Adventurer, you whose weight is borne by your winged soul! The mystical world of Theldesia is home to dragons and giants, magical beasts, and demihumans. Fragrant green winds blow across this new yet ancient land that opens before you like a blank page. Fill it with your life.

L**O**G HORIZON

1 THE BEGINNING OF ANOTHER WORLD

MAMARE TOUNO   ILLUSTRATION BY **KAZUHIRO HARA**

YEN
ON

NEW YORK

PROLOGUE

"Naotsugu, look out! Up ahead on your right!"

"Bring it! I've got this."

Naotsugu yelled back to Shiroe, raising his shield. The shield gleamed dull silver as he brought it down on a Triffid.

"My liege!"

Checking a writhing green vine that had darted out from the left with a single swift strike, Akatsuki slid into a low crouch, positioned to guard Shiroe.

Smallstone Herb Garden wasn't a large zone. However, the ancient gaming facility within its boundaries meant the topography was more varied than the surrounding ruins, and this made it a difficult place to fight.

"...Hey, how come there are so many of these things?"

"They multiply every time you say something off-color, Naotsugu."

"What, it's *my* fault?!"

Instead of answering, Shiroe generated a pale magic arrow and fired it into a Brier Weasel. Mind Bolt, an arrow of psychic power that could go right through single enemies, was one of the basic offensive spells for Enchanters. Even as he watched the meter-long weasel jump with a piercing shriek, Shiroe mentally visualized an icon. Since recast time was in effect, the icon had lost all its color and was slowly refilling like an hourglass. Shiroe wouldn't be able to use that spell again until the icon had regained its glow. It didn't matter. He had nearly thirty other spells at his command.

"Rush them! Akatsuki, you take the left flank!"

"Yes, sir!"

"On it!"

In any case, even if he hadn't been able to use his spells, Shiroe had two companions on his side now.

"Better get ready 'cos here I come! Shield Smash!"

The silver-armored warrior charging down the moss-covered path, sweeping his shield from side to side, was Naotsugu. He was a tall guy with short hair and bright, lively eyes, and he and Shiroe had been friends for years. His class was Guardian. The three Warrior classes specialized in single-handedly fielding enemy attacks, and of the three, Guardians had the highest Defense. In *Elder Tales*, they boasted the nickname "The Unbreakable Shield."

"…Too slow."

A girl who had the air of a swallow about her darted through the space Naotsugu's advance had cleared. A grotesque creature like a split rugby ball with glass fangs sprang at her, but the girl cut it down with her short sword as she ran, not even pausing. This was Akatsuki: a slight girl whose black hair danced in the wind. Also Shiroe's friend, she felt no qualms about calling him "my liege." She was an Assassin, a type of master swordsman whose techniques included a one-strike kill and which boasted the greatest physical attack force of all twelve classes.

Even as he admired their work, Shiroe hurried after them.

Shiroe's class was Enchanter. Of the three Magician classes, Enchanters were a complete support class that specialized in support spells and negative status magic. As with all the Magician classes, their Defense was shaky. Shiroe couldn't even wear the Adventurer's leather armor Akatsuki wore, let alone Naotsugu's sturdy full armor. All he had under his big white mantle, which looked a bit like a lab coat, were an ordinary tunic shirt and trousers.

Since Shiroe was a rear guard player with poor Defense, it wasn't a good idea for him to be alone on a battlefield. That said, considering the enemy's ranged attack spells, it was dangerous for him to get too close to the front line, too. The best policy was for him to leave a certain distance between himself and Naotsugu and Akatsuki while keeping a wary eye out for sneak attacks from the rear.

As field zones went, Smallstone Herb Garden wasn't all that difficult. The monsters that appeared here—Triffids, Brier Weasels, Venom Moths—were level 50 at most.

Shiroe, Akatsuki, and Naotsugu were all level-90 Adventurers. Their abilities were nearly the highest rank possible in the world of the MMORPG *Elder Tales*. Shiroe's Defense might be low, but with a level difference like this one, he wouldn't take damage easily.

In any case, although Naotsugu had said there were a lot, any one of the three could have kicked ten or twenty Triffid-level enemies to pieces all on their own.

…Well, yes. We're fine for now… But.

For a while now, Naotsugu and Akatsuki had been bantering as if they didn't need all their attention for the fight, but their faces were serious.

Battles were a terrifying thing.

Even if their bodies were enhanced, even if they were able to use spells and sword skills at the touch of an icon, terror was a constant companion when they faced down monsters. The legs planted firmly on the ground, the hands that held his staff at the ready—this was Shiroe's real body. All of this belonged to him: the wind that brushed his cheek, the raucous howls of the monsters, and the adrenaline rushing through his veins. It was harder than he'd imagined to block or to absorb damage from the claws and fangs that were suddenly right in front of him or the flames and gobs of acid that flew at him. The three of them had determined that the only way to overcome this fear was experience, and lots of it.

"On your right!"

"I see it."

His face grim, Naotsugu quickly checked the direction Shiroe had warned him about, then struck with the longsword he held in his right hand. The attack missed its mark, but it seemed to have deterred the Brier Weasel. Bristling with green spines, the weasel glared with bloodred eyes and gave a few throaty howls, backing away.

The attack hadn't been an exception.

As level-90 Adventurers, it shouldn't even have been possible for an attack they made against a level-48 monster to fail. Here, too, Shiroe could see the gaps in their teamwork. They still hadn't done enough training together.

Their bodies might be level 90, but they didn't yet have full control of their abilities.

In that case, Shiroe concluded, he should respond accordingly. He cast a ranged spell.

"Nightmare Sphere!"

Nightmare Sphere was an Enchanter's ranged attack spell. That said, it couldn't do much damage. Enchanters weren't good with damage spells to begin with. Compared to other classes at the same level, the offensive spells they could cast on their own were notoriously weak. As if to prove this, although the spell Shiroe had launched flew in an unsteady arc to touch down and burst in the midst of the weasels and prowling plants, it didn't seem to have done much damage.

It would take him more than one attack to beat a monster even half his level. The only attack methods the Enchanter class had were low-damage ones. It was one of the things that made Enchanter a pretty unpopular class in *Elder Tales*.

When it came to games, gamers were quite callous. In the program—a world ruled by formulas—numbers were everything. True, it was just a game. Still, precisely *because* it was a game, the society inside it was all the more ruthlessly stratified. There was a huge difference between the reputations of the popular classes, which were rumored to get preferential treatment, and the unpopular classes.

However, even if it had a poor reputation with the average gamer, Shiroe had no complaints about his class. It was probably very nice to have superior abilities, but since he didn't have them, he saw more benefit in arranging things so he could enjoy himself without them. That was how Shiroe played, and he'd never been inconvenienced by it.

Besides, Shiroe liked Enchanters. He liked the way things never seemed to go their way. He liked the fact that they were weak. He also liked the huge potential they held. Shiroe's weakness was being unable to do anything on his own. The Enchanter design concept held the flip side of that weakness. That was what had attracted him to it.

Shiroe's Nightmare Sphere unleashed a transparent psychic wave across its attack range. The dozen or so monsters inside the range were caught up in that wave, and the shock slowed their movements to a crawl. While it lasted, which wouldn't be long, Nightmare Sphere's effect caused a negative move speed reduction status in its targets.

Two cheerful voices rang out.

"Hey, yeah! That'll be easy to hit!"

"Thank you, my liege."

Although the enemies they were currently fighting—Triffids and Brier Weasels—looked grotesque and daunting in the extreme, none of them measured more than a meter or so. In terms of attack reach, Naotsugu and Akatsuki's swords gave them an overwhelming advantage. With the monsters' speed reduced, all they had to do was walk right up to them and make sure their attacks hit home.

"There we go! One down!"

"Likewise."

"Not bad, short stuff!"

"Do *not* call me short stuff, stupid Naotsugu!"

Of course, his friends weren't the type to dwell on gloom and doom. Naotsugu was more cheerful and tougher than average, and although Akatsuki was normally a girl of few words, she could hold her own against Naotsugu with room to spare.

One opportunity and a little assist, and in the blink of an eye they'd started to take the monsters out. Shiroe followed behind, acting as support. All he had to do was use a spell to bind the occasional monster they'd missed and lob an attack at it.

Knowing that speed reduction would put them at an advantage in battle, Shiroe had developed his own system. He used binding spells like Nightmare Sphere and Astral Bind to limit enemy abilities, then focused on assisting the vanguard. It was nothing, if you thought about it. Just a basic fighting strategy, one he'd used a thousand times before.

Well, we can't waste too much time and energy on low-ranking monsters like these, he thought. *There's a formation I want to test today.*

"One, two, and gone!"

"Hup!"

Two sharp yells. Naotsugu and Akatsuki were both veteran players. One cue was all it had taken for them to shift into teamwork-focused combo plays. By now, there was no trace of the confusion they'd shown earlier.

"Was that the last of 'em?"

Naotsugu swung his one-handed sword energetically, then wiped off the blood and slid it into its sheath.

Shiroe nodded. At some point, while his mind had been elsewhere, the battle had ended. He lowered his staff and canceled the spells he'd had on standby.

"We took out a lot of them."

"I don't see any more enemies in the area. It's probably a good idea to keep an eye out, though. —Would you two mind doing the retrieval on your own?"

With that, Shiroe began acting as lookout. The warning icon in the back of his mind had changed from red to a calm marine blue, signaling that the battle was truly over. Naotsugu and Akatsuki were gathering loot from the fallen monsters. They were probably planning to strip off the pelts.

These were survival instincts they'd acquired over the past few weeks.

Fortunately, the sun was still high. If some emergency came up, he wasn't likely to miss it. Shiroe took a canteen out of the magic bag at his waist, drank a mouthful, and listened carefully, on the alert. *You know, really... I'm the gloomiest one here.*

He heaved a deep sigh.

When he looked down, he saw the white hem of his mantle. Trousers made of thick cloth, meant for outdoor wear, but of fine quality. Short, soft, comfortable boots, which, if memory served him right, were made of Thunder Elk leather.

In his hands, incredibly, he held a staff.

The Staff of the Wise Horned Owl—a rare item that increased spell power and chanting speed and one of Shiroe's greatest assets. At two meters long, it was taller than Shiroe himself. Its design was mystical and rather striking. He thought it looked cool, but it wasn't the sort of "cool" that belonged to the real world. It was the sort found only in games.

Nothing had been the same since the day of what Shiroe and the others had begun to call "the Catastrophe."

Another reality, one with no heroic grandeur or softened edges. Cynical, muddy, and endlessly harsh.

This reality was the monsters they'd been fighting a few minutes ago. It was the lush green of the crumbling ruins where he stood, straining his ears. It was the dull *thwack* of a hatchet being brought down, over and over, as his friends dismembered their kills. It was the chill wind that blew through the forest, and it was the terror of battle that still prickled under his skin.

All this was now part of the "reality" Shiroe belonged to.

Elder Tales was—or used to be—just a game. Ever since the day of the Catastrophe, when everything had changed, Shiroe and the others seemed to have been locked inside it.

Still, we can fight. We just did. Fighting earns us a few gold coins, and there are beds waiting for us. I met up with Naotsugu and Akatsuki, too. When you look at it that way, we're actually really lucky.

Shiroe caught himself in the middle of a sigh; his thoughts had begun to turn dark, and he forced them onto a different track. He could visualize the day of the Catastrophe. Countless players cowering in the streets of Akiba. He didn't want to let himself sink into a swamp of apathy the way they had.

Even as Shiroe scanned his surroundings, alert for signs of movement, he let his mind run back to the day the Catastrophe had occurred.

CHAPTER.

1

"CATASTROPHE"

► LEVEL: **90**

► RACE: **HALF ALV**

► CLASS: **ENCHANTER**

► HP: **8303**

► MP: **12088**

► ITEM 1:

[STAFF OF THE WISE HORNED OWL]

A STAFF INFUSED WITH THE DIVINE PROTECTION OF THE HORNED OWL, MESSENGER OF THE GODDESS OF WISDOM. ITS WISDOM ILLUMINATES THE DARKNESS AND IS SAID TO AID ITS BEARER'S THOUGHTS. BOOSTS SPELL FORCE AND INCREASES CHANTING SPEED.

► ITEM 2:

[SACRED ROBE OF THE STARS]

MADE OF CLOTH WOVEN FROM THE TRACKS OF FALLING STARS. WORN ONLY BY MAGIC USERS. AN ULTRARARE CREATED ITEM THAT REQUIRES FANTASY-CLASS MATERIALS. RECEIVES POWER FROM THE LOCATIONS OF THE STARS AND ENHANCES THE FORCE OF ASTRAL ATTACK SPELLS.

► ITEM 3:

[THE KAH OF THE MILLENNIAL BIRD]

A LEGENDARY TALISMAN CARVED FROM A FRAGMENT THAT BURST FROM THE SACRED TREE VENDELIA WHEN A SACRED BIRD WAS BORN FROM IT. IT HAS DOMINION OVER INDESTRUCTIBLE LIFE AND REDUCES THE EFFECT OF MOVE INTERFERENCE NEGATIVE STATUSES.

<Map>
A must-have item for lost
players. You can't draw one if
you're lost, though.

Shiroe rounded a stump several meters tall that was just where he'd imagined it would be, then turned the corner of a two-story building that was exactly where he'd remembered. The ground was carpeted with green moss, and only a few scattered patches of the old asphalt showed through. He was running through a bristling forest of ruins, the buildings choked and pierced by enormous, ancient trees. It was the first time he'd seen this place directly, but he had seen it before, and he ran as if he were flying.

There were figures huddled by the roadside. Adventurers in the same boat as Shiroe. Their screams and moans forcibly quelled the terror that had clawed its way up his throat.

It was ego, pure and simple.

"What *is* this?!"

"I-I... This can't be right... What's going on?!"

"S-somebody, get over here! Hey! Admin! I know you can hear me!!"

Their yells sounded like the shrieks of dying animals. The sheer wretchedness of it all helped Shiroe hang on to the ghost of his presence of mind. He didn't want to start screaming like that. The feeling was all that kept Shiroe running.

My body's moving the way I tell it to. My arms and legs aren't quite the right size; that's why it feels weird... Good thing it wasn't a huge difference.

The town of Akiba spread out before him.

Akiba: hometown to many players and the largest city on the Japanese *Elder Tales* server. A riot of vines grew through the asphalt, twining around and through the jumble of ruined buildings. The buildings seemed to fuse with trees that were older than time and blessed by the spirits. Shiroe knew the place so well he felt something akin to homesickness for it.

"Akiba? —Like hell! Have I gone nuts?! Somebody, anybody, answer me!" The men crouched nearby were yelling. Every last one of them was dressed like someone from a medieval fantasy world, in armor or loose cloth robes.

That was only natural. *Elder Tales* was the world's largest massively multiplayer online game, set in a world of sword and sorcery.

But it was supposed to be just a game.

The wind that rushed past Shiroe's cheeks was cold and damp and brisk, as if he was deep in the forest. It was nothing like the dry, astringent air of Tokyo, where he really lived. The green scent on the wind told him that, wherever he was, it wasn't the world he knew.

Shiroe gave his head a shake, thinking back. He'd been playing *Elder Tales*. He remembered sitting at home, at his desk, immersed in the game unfolding on the LCD monitor.

Elder Tales was a venerable, old game that had been around for twenty years. The content and rendering engines had been updated to the latest versions time and time again, of course, but it was the treasure trove of data and the sheer depth the game had acquired over its long run that made it such a hit with users.

Today was supposed to have been a red-letter day: the application date for the twelfth *Elder Tales* expansion pack. Today, data that players had downloaded in advance would be unlocked, giving the world of *Elder Tales* new items and zones, new monsters and battles, and—most important of all—raising the level maximum.

Since it was the day of the expansion pack introduction, there were bound to have been a ton of players linked to the game world. Shiroe had no way to check the actual numbers, but he could see from his friend list that many of his comrades had been online.

Shiroe was a veteran *Elder Tales* player. He'd been playing the game for eight years, ever since middle school.

This gigantic network game had more than 100,000 fans in Japan alone. Worldwide, more than twenty million people were crazy about it, and it had fascinated Shiroe for a very long time.

Of course Shiroe had been looking forward to the new expansion pack, too, but the idea of acting like a giddy newbie embarrassed him, so he'd decided to just play the way he normally did. He'd been looking out for a pair of twins lately. From what he could remember, he'd gone to a beginner's area to help them practice hunting, given them a little advice, and had been telling them about items.

At that point, there was a yawning gap in his memory.

He seemed to recall watching some sort of demo.

Letters of flame gleaming on a black screen.

A sky brimming with sticky asphalt darkness that scrolled past at ferocious speed, with a white moon like a hole cut out of the blackness.

…And that was all.

Now he was here, running through the streets of Akiba, real legs—his own legs—pounding the ground.

A lilting tone, like xylophone notes, rang in his ears. The familiar chime signaled the arrival of a telechat. Shiroe narrowed his eyes, concentrating his attention on his forehead, and chose "Select" from the menu that appeared in his mind's eye. He'd learned that particular operation just after being dropped into this game world, as soon as he'd gotten over the initial panic.

"Shiro, where are you?"

"Almost there."

With his old friend's voice in his ears, Shiroe turned right again, rounding the corner of another ruined building that looked ready to come tumbling down.

There was a damp smell on the gentle wind. The wind made a clear, brisk sound as it brushed through the treetops. And that bright light… It was the weightless sort of light that only appears in early summer. There in the chilly wind, rather than the heat of sunlight, it seemed to be an endless white blast, pure and overwhelming in its intensity. Under that early summer light, the ancient trees and buildings cast jet-black shadows on the dark soil and asphalt of the avenue. The contrast was beautiful.

The landscape that spread out before Shiroe was Akiba, his hometown in the game world. He'd seen it too many times to count, but now it completely enveloped him, bringing with it an overpowering sense of reality that was beyond the capacity of any game.

He was there, running through the middle of it on his own two feet. With every step, he felt himself slide as the wet moss crumbled beneath his shoes. He could feel his heart pushing blood into every last corner of his exercise-warmed body.

This was undeniably reality.

The town of Akiba was just as Shiroe remembered it. The buildings that seemed on the verge of crumbling, the barracks tavern with its many annexes that had been built at different times, the great trees with roots that ran across the road… This was the Akiba of the game: The sacred ground of an ancient people, coexisting with the green forest even as it slowly sank into it. A hometown for players in the eastern area of the crescent-shaped archipelago Yamato, it was located in Eastal, the League of Free Cities, and was the central city of the Japanese *Elder Tales* server.

Shiroe ran down the central avenue, turning at the corner of a three-story combination inn and tavern. The crumbling ruins were concrete buildings. All sorts of buildings and landmarks from the real-world Akihabara—SUFTEC, Yashikayama Electric, Kuruta Tower—had been recreated inside *Elder Tales* as ruins from another century.

Sleeping remnants of that ancient time were scattered all over this world. Some were enormous underground ruins, others were towers that soared into the sky, and still others were towns like Akiba.

It was a strange sight: A log annex clinging to a gigantic concrete structure that had nearly turned to rubble, and all of it wrapped in the embrace of an ancient tree. As Shiroe reached his destination, Naotsugu got up from where he'd been sitting on a fallen chunk of concrete and came to meet him. The light that angled in through the gaping windows, long empty of glass, shone down on the two with a crystal clarity impossible for any game screen to render.

Naotsugu's face was pale, but even so, he grinned and smacked the hilt of his sword. He had a sturdy build and stood a bit over

180 centimeters. Right now, he looked for all the world like a battle-hardened warrior: He was wearing steel armor that looked formidably tough, if plain, and he carried a shield on his back.

"Hey, Shiro!"

"Naotsugu. I, uh… Good morning."

Shiroe didn't know quite how to respond to Naotsugu's greeting, and he ended up sounding brusque.

The standard version of *Elder Tales* was equipped with a voice chat function that let players talk to their friends while they gamed, using a microphone and speaker connected to their computer. Some users didn't like audio chats, preferring to type instead, but Shiroe and Naotsugu hadn't been among them. That meant Shiroe was very familiar with Naotsugu's voice.

Naotsugu Hasegawa. When anyone asked Shiroe whom he could count on in this game, that was one of the first names that came to mind.

Online games are played over the Internet, and *Elder Tales* belonged to the massively multiplayer (or multiuser) category. In these games, anywhere between several hundred and several thousand users access the same game space and play simultaneously. In other words, the games are designed to let players encounter throngs of other players in the game world and either cooperate or compete with them. Shiroe had played *Elder Tales* for many years, and naturally, he had quite a few acquaintances in the game.

However, acquaintances made in the game world tended to stay there. Although it depended on play styles and individual mind-sets, almost no users played under their real identities. Network crimes had continued to rise since the year 2000, and protecting personal information was just common sense, something one did in order to survive in an online society.

That didn't mean it was impossible to make real friends.

Naotsugu knew Shiroe's real name. He was one of the few players to whom Shiroe had given his real-world contact information, and they'd even met outside the game in real life.

…All of which meant that hearing Naotsugu's voice was a relief to Shiroe. He was one of the players Shiroe was closest to in *Elder Tales*. Although they'd met off-line a few times, they'd blown far, far more time on dumb conversations held online through their monitors.

As members of the Debauchery Tea Party, Shiroe and Naotsugu had spent countless days and nights traveling to endless outlying zones and plunging through battles together.

They'd had all sorts of empty-headed conversations. They'd even had confidential talks about trivial things, the sort of talks that made the friendship seem too close to have been formed through a game.

To Shiroe, this cheerful, reliable voice meant "Naotsugu."

"So what's the deal? Did *Elder Tales* actually evolve this far while I was gone? It's so awesome it's kind of a turnoff. I don't think you could do all this by improving particle systems or rendering engines. Could you? I mean, is this some kind of joke?"

Naotsugu's big mouth was set in an irritated line. Even that cheerful voice of his, the one that was always talking back, seemed a bit gray and subdued.

"Seriously, this is out of my league. I give up."

Shiroe nodded vaguely, then raised the staff he held.

...*Check that out. It's a staff. An actual staff.*

The staff was the sort commonly found in fantasy games: made of wood, taller than Shiroe, and quite obviously meant for a Magician. It looked as though someone had taken a gnarled branch, polished it up, and added decorative metal bits for reinforcement. Anyone who wanted to see something like this in the real world would have had to go to a costume shop.

Possibly because he'd picked up on Shiroe's silent gesture, Naotsugu looked down at himself. He was wearing heavy-duty steel armor that looked as if it weighed several dozen kilos. He carried a shield on his back, and there was a sword in the embellished sheath that hung at his side. He could have been a warrior straight out of a fantasy tale.

"...Well, I guess I look like a cosplayer, too."

"Yes. Yes, you do."

They both laughed, and although you couldn't have called it cheerful laughter, it wasn't subdued, either.

"You know, though... You really look like yourself."

"So do you."

Each of them looked the other over carefully. Fundamentally, both looked like their *Elder Tales* game characters, but the original characters had been polygon graphics, far from photo-realistic. Now, both were physically there and as detailed as reality.

A closer look revealed that the game hadn't simply been translated to real life. Both the male and female characters in *Elder Tales* had been designed to be good-looking. The slick modeling was a natural marketing response to user demand: Very few users would willingly pay money to play a game in which they were homely.

That said, Naotsugu didn't just look like a real version of his handsome *Elder Tales* polygon model. Shiroe could see traces of the real-world Naotsugu, the one he'd met several times.

"Your face looks kinda like you, Naotsugu."

The striking vertical scar that had bisected one of the game character's eyebrows was gone, and he could make out the real Naotsugu's bright eyes, tilted slightly downward at the outer corners, and the boyish smile that made him seem younger than he was.

"You, too, Shiro. You've got that creepy *sanpaku*-eyes thing going, so it's like you're always glaring, and you look like some kind of honor student with those glasses."

Shiroe had heard similar things about his face from acquaintances for as long as he could remember. Apparently they were true for this version of it, too. Shiroe tossed his usual response Naotsugu's way: "Just drop it, all right?"

"What's actually going on? If you know anything, spill it, you shifty Machiavelli-with-glasses."

"I'd love to tell you, but I've got no idea."

Shiroe didn't have much information on the current situation, either.

Shiroe and Naotsugu had kicked away the scattered chunks of concrete and were sitting down. This building was much closer to the center of Akiba than the area on the outskirts of town where Shiroe had woken up a short while ago. If he listened hard, he could hear the uproar from the city center as a faint murmur.

"Well, first off… This isn't a dream. Right?"
"Right."
Shiroe nodded.

When he'd come to, he'd found himself in a familiar place, but it wasn't a place that existed in reality. It seemed to be the world of the game he knew like the back of his hand. *Elder Tales* was set in a world of sword and sorcery, which players journeyed through using Adventurer characters they'd created as alter egos. The body Shiroe currently inhabited was the one the game character Shiroe had used.

That said, it seemed to have acquired a resemblance to the real-world Shiroe.

"What about your status?"

"I checked."

Because *Elder Tales* was a game, Adventurers were equipped with various quantified abilities, such as physical strength and stamina. In the game, players used icons to select status displays for their abilities and every possible action from a menu.

In this world, a simple look around showed no signs of any game-related display. However, if they focused their attention on their foreheads, a range of data displays and icons appeared, layered over whatever they were looking at. Within thirty minutes after regaining consciousness, both Naotsugu and Shiroe had discovered that they could mentally move the cursors to select items.

Immediately afterward, they'd noticed the telechat function. This function could be used to contact friends who were also playing the game but were far away. In other words, it was the *Elder Tales* version of a cell phone. However, it could only be used with acquaintances registered to a player's friend list.

When Shiroe—concentrating on his forehead and struggling desperately with the unfamiliar operations—had discovered Naotsugu's name on his friend list, he'd been so startled and glad to see it that he'd yelled aloud. Naotsugu had been surprised when Shiroe contacted him, but he'd readily agreed to meet at a nearby ruin.

"........."

"........."

Silence. Both Shiroe and Naotsugu were thinking of what to tell the other and where to start, but the answer was already clear. Shiroe probably knew a bit more about the circumstances than Naotsugu. As far as Shiroe knew, Naotsugu hadn't accessed *Elder Tales* for two years.

Shiroe told Naotsugu everything he knew, although that wasn't much. There were all sorts of things he could tell Naotsugu about the two years he'd been away from the game, but Shiroe knew nothing about the background or cause of the impossible incident they'd gotten caught up in.

He knew they'd been about to introduce the new expansion pack, *Homesteading the Noosphere*. He knew he'd been playing with some newbies near the city when he'd gotten dragged into this mess. He knew that this place looked just like the town of Akiba, his starting point in *Elder Tales*, that they seemed to have the bodies of their game characters, and that they'd inherited the characters' equipment and items as well.

Come to think of it, I wonder what happened to the twins? —I'll have to check on them later.

He also knew he knew nothing at all about whatever had caused all this.

While Shiroe talked, Naotsugu listened quietly. He asked questions about a few topics he wasn't familiar with, but he didn't interrupt with his own ideas.

Shiroe wasn't partial to noise. Not that he hated it when things were lively; he just didn't like chaotic uproar. Naotsugu may have been cheerful and easily carried away, but he wasn't such an idiot that he couldn't listen when people were talking. Their personalities were different, but—possibly because each had enough leeway to match the other's pace—they got along surprisingly well.

"...Huhn. Hm. A different world, huh? —Some other world, and we got sucked in. Everything turned real..."

"What were you doing here, Naotsugu? You came back?" Shiroe asked.

"Yeah. I heard about the new expansion pack. Things had settled down at work, and I thought I'd log in and see what was up."

—A comeback.

Naotsugu came back, Shiroe thought. *He was trying to come back...*

If he recalled correctly, Naotsugu was two years older than he was. They'd met about four years ago. By then, Shiroe had already been a senior *Elder Tales* player. Guys who'd been messing with computers since middle school weren't rare, but even among them, Shiroe was an extreme indoors type. Specifically, even when he went outdoors, he was mentally indoors: a kid who always managed to be on his own, even in a crowd.

He moved on to high school, then to college, but his interests stayed the same, and there was hardly a day when he didn't journey through virtual space.

By that time, *Elder Tales* already had a certain special standing among online games. It was so good that gamers told other gamers, "If you want to play a really solid game, play *Elder Tales*."

For example, *Elder Tales* housed the Half-Gaia Project, a crazy-sounding plan on a mind-boggling scale. It was a project to create a half-sized version of Earth.

The town of Akiba, the initial starting point for players on the Japanese server, was located in Tokyo's spot on the Japanese archipelago. The initial starting points on the North American server were Big Apple and South Angel. The terms "Japanese server" and "North American server" were just for convenience's sake: The unified network formed by the multiple servers that connected to these two made it theoretically possible to journey to a different continent or the ends of the earth. In other words, it was possible to immigrate to another server. This was a tough thing to do in regular MMO games, and it was one of *Elder Tales*'s selling points. Of course, the Half-Gaia Project was a very long-term goal, and at present, the in-game Gaia wasn't a complete replica of the world.

In *Elder Tales*, the world was divided up into zones. A zone was a unit used to express area or range within games. There were vast field zones haunted by vicious monsters like the Fuji Sea of Trees, dungeon zones that acted as the stage for adventures like the ruined Shinjuku station building, and noncombat areas like the Akiba urban zone. There were even tiny zones the size of hotel rooms. Some zones were available for purchase and could be bought by a player who'd saved up enough in-game currency.

The zones were connected to each other in various ways. Since the borders between field zones were invisible, with one zone flowing seamlessly into the next, players tended not to pay much attention to exactly which zone they were in. If one was on the move, they'd cross into the next zone long before noticing. Other zones were sometimes clearly partitioned. For example, if a building or room acted as an independent zone, it was normal for a door or gateway to function as the threshold between zones.

To the best of Shiroe's knowledge, the Japanese server already administered several hundred thousand zones, and the developer had spread the game all over the world through multiple subcontractors. In a game this vast, players like Shiroe who'd been around for years and had commensurate knowledge were considered reliable and convenient. As a result, over the course of his gaming career, Shiroe had been approached by all sorts of guilds. He'd joined one for a short while, just to see what it was like.

Guilds were teams of multiple players, and the most common type of community in *Elder Tales*. Players who joined a guild were given access to an exclusive guild account at the in-game bank, were able to use safe-deposit boxes for easier item receipt and delivery, and could take advantage of several convenient services. It was easier for guild members to contact one another and to put together parties when leaving on an adventure. Belonging to a guild was convenient and profitable, and as a result, many of the players in *Elder Tales* joined up.

Shiroe had always been the type to get totally immersed in whatever interested him, and on top of that, he'd read everything he could find on the overseas versions of *Elder Tales*. Even among players who'd been around for the same length of time, he had an exceptional amount of knowledge. No doubt the guilds had seen him as a useful recruit.

No single player had a perfect grasp of the game's innumerable zones. Even Shiroe's memory couldn't handle that much information. Still, just knowing about the main traffic routes, the way various zones were linked together, and the Fairy Ring transport devices was enough to shorten travel time. It was also important to constantly accumulate knowledge on what sort of items were sold in which zone and what sort of monsters appeared where.

Elder Tales was an imaginary world created from a jumble of innumerable zones that held countless types of items and monsters, commissioned adventures known as "quests," all sorts of folklore and ancient knowledge, and an enormous assortment of other elements that the developers had dreamed up.

However, Shiroe hadn't been able to get used to relationships built around convenience and profit and loss. He'd grown up a bit now, but at the time, Shiroe had been far more willful, still very much a kid, and—embarrassingly—obsessively conscientious.

Shiroe wasn't good at relying on people, but he wasn't bad at being relied on by others.

Just because he wasn't bad at it didn't mean it didn't hurt.

Online games attract all sorts of people. Where there are people, there are human relationships, and not all of those relationships are pretty. There are countless ugly ones as well, and they were too much for a middle schooler like Shiroe.

A little while after joining the guild, Shiroe realized that the people around him were using him as their own personal solutions site. Even though Shiroe's level was already high, he was being shuffled this way and that like a jack-of-all-trades and loaned out to help other players battle. Shiroe couldn't get used to that sort of relationship, and he wasn't able to deal with the other members. He'd left the guild and, ever since, had stuck to temporary relationships or adventured on his own.

Before he knew it, Shiroe had become a lone wolf. Since he had quite a lot of knowledge and level status for a loner, he'd also become fairly well-known, and as if in proportion to the notoriety, he'd become a rather jaded player.

Shiroe had met Naotsugu after his skills had improved and after he'd given up on guild ties and journeyed alone for a while, just about the time he'd grown numb to the loneliness. They'd met at the notorious Debauchery Tea Party.

The Debauchery Tea Party was not a guild. It was the Debauchery Tea Party, no more, no less; there really were no other words to describe it. To an objective spectator, it looked like nothing more than an accidental group of players who'd just happened to be there. Even if they "just happened to be there," though, they *were* there, always, at any time. —That was Shiroe and his friends.

They were from all sorts of guilds.
Their personalities were all over the place.
They had nothing whatsoever in common.

Even so, Shiroe and the others met sometimes in ruined buildings, sometimes out on the plains, sometimes on hills under a sky of falling stars.

They met, and they adventured.

Elder Tales was a medieval sword-and-sorcery fantasy. There was an idea—so common among players that it was practically treated as official background—that the *Elder Tales* world probably came a few thousand years after the present-day world. According to the in-game folklore, an enormous war had broken out and destroyed the world, which had then been miraculously rebuilt by the gods. It was a pretty common fantasy game creation myth.

Of course, the world swarmed with all the usual monsters: orcs and goblins, trolls and hill giants, Chimeras and Hydras. Most of players enjoyed battles. Fighting monsters, earning experience points, leveling up, and acquiring rare and powerful items was the most common way to play *Elder Tales*.

However, that was "battling" and "getting items." It wasn't "adventuring." The Debauchery Tea Party was where Shiroe had first learned that fighting battle after battle and adventuring were completely different things.

Then, too, *she* had been a regular fixture at the Debauchery Tea Party, along with friends who supported her. Shiroe had been a solid part of that group.

At the Debauchery Tea Party, Shiroe had found what were probably his very first friends in *Elder Tales*. One of those friends had been Naotsugu.

▶ **2**

"If you were thinking about coming back, had things calmed down at work?"

"Yeah. Finally. I tell ya, it was a crazy year."

The Debauchery Tea Party had been active for two years. Those two years were the happiest, most fulfilling years of all the time Shiroe had spent in *Elder Tales*. However, due to a variety of overlapping circumstances, the Debauchery Tea Party had closed its doors, leaving several legends in its wake.

One of the triggers had been Naotsugu's departure from the game. One winter, things had gotten busy at Naotsugu's company, and he'd had to stop gaming for a while. As luck would have it, several other members had also had to leave the game around that time due to personal matters.

The Debauchery Tea Party hadn't been a guild. Since it wasn't a guild, none of the relationships in it had been formed around shallow profit and loss. Although they were all old enough to be embarrassed by the idea and would never have said it aloud, Shiroe and the other members had really treasured one another.

That was why the Debauchery Tea Party had suspended its activities indefinitely, even though no one had specifically suggested this. They'd considered inviting new friends and keeping the Tea Party open, of course, but that would have been another adventure, another story.

It had been sad to see the group dissolve, but none of the members hung their heads and mourned. They'd shared lots of adventures and enjoyed themselves more than anyone else. That was compensation enough.

"I finally got used to the job; thanks for asking. It's been going pretty well, actually… I guess one thing does have me worried: There's not a single cute girl at my company."

"Big deal. Who cares about that?"

Shiroe shrugged off Naotsugu's complaint.

If ever there was a good guy, it was Naotsugu. In terms of true grit, Shiroe was confident that Naotsugu was much braver than he was. Sometimes he was *too* brave. Shiroe couldn't recall a single situation that had been enough to stop Naotsugu from joking around.

"What's with the glare? Moody perv."

"I'm not a moody perv."

"No, trust me, you're a moody perv. There are two types of guy in the world: liberated, 'open' pervs and introverted, moody pervs. I'm the open kind, and I love girls' panties. You're the moody kind, and I know—*know*—that you love panties, too."

Shiroe grimaced at that outrageous theory… Not that he was actually upset.

For as long as he'd known him, Naotsugu had picked up on the atmosphere in situations and tossed oddball topics like that one around to lighten the mood. Besides, although he'd rather not deal with anything too glaringly raunchy, Shiroe was a healthy, young adult male and not entirely uninterested in the opposite sex. He liked to think he wasn't narrow-minded enough to let a petty line like that one make him mad.

"Well, yeah, I— I mean, sure, I like girls, but I wouldn't take just *any* girl."

"Hey, I know what's inside the package is what's important. I just don't think there's anything wrong with getting worked up over the package, too, you know? …But under the circumstances…"

Naotsugu heaved a big sigh.

"Yeah."

Shiroe nodded. He knew all too well what Naotsugu meant.

"Work may have calmed down a bit, but I sure didn't ask for a vacation in some other world," Naotsugu cracked, trying to make light of the situation. "Seriously, are we even gonna be able to get back?"

All of the countless players who'd gotten dragged into this world were no doubt asking themselves that exact same question. The fact that Naotsugu was able to joke about a question that was so heavy it made it hard to breathe just went to show how mentally tough he was and how considerate he was toward Shiroe.

"I think what we have here is one god stepping down and another one taking over. The new god has the brain of a delusional thirteen-year-old."

"Talk about a grim situation. Just look at all this. The world's gone completely around the bend. What kind of a party is this, anyway?!"

"Right. It's probably best to assume we won't be going home anytime soon."

"…And a merciless view of said grim situation. Wonderful."

"Only people who want to die add mercy to grim situations."

"Now *that* sounds like the Tea Party strategy counselor I know," Naotsugu wisecracked.

He shook his head a few times as if resetting his mood, then continued, his expression more serious. "All right. For now, I'll give up…

So, what next? This is one of those stock fantasy novel situations, and we're going to have to survive from here on out, right?"

Shiroe nodded reluctantly. From what he could remember, he hadn't done anything out of the ordinary. He'd gone through his daily routine, taken a bath as usual, logged in to *Elder Tales* as usual, practiced hunting with the new twin players he'd met the other day, then been knocked out by something he hadn't seen coming. He couldn't remember anything else. He'd been doing pretty much the same things he usually did when he'd been forcibly pulled into this world, or dragged into this situation. There might have been some sort of cause or error on his part in there somewhere, but under the circumstances, there was no way of knowing.

In addition, even if there was some way to get out of this other world (or situation), Shiroe didn't know what it was, at least not right now.

That meant that, whether they managed to find a way to get back to the world they'd left or simply waited to be sent back by the same sort of accident that had pulled them into this world in the first place, they'd have to survive here until it happened.

"It's possible that we'll wake up back in our world if we die here, but I wouldn't recommend trying it. It would be a little like those guys who are sure the world's going to end, so they go and borrow a hundred million yen from a loan shark."

"Yeah, it doesn't sound like a genius move. If we really just died, we'd just be dead. Loser city."

"Exactly."

"Still, we shouldn't have much of a problem with the survival part. Right, Counselor Shiro?"

"You don't think so?"

"Well, no. We're level ninety. We might have a problem getting through a super-tough zone, but if we're talking about just surviving, it shouldn't be that hard. We've even got money. Equipment, too... Mine's kinda old, but it'll do. See? No problem."

The *Elder Tales* RPG included a level system. At level 90, Shiroe and Naotsugu had reached the highest level there was, but it didn't make them exceptional. Almost half the game's players were at level 90. *Elder Tales* had a long history, and like most online games, it had added several hundred expansion packs with all sorts of new elements over the course of that history. Shiroe hadn't experienced it firsthand, but he'd heard that when *Elder Tales* was first released, the highest level had been 50. Fans had loved the game, and they'd wanted to keep adventuring even after they'd hit level 50. An expansion pack had been released in response to the demand; in addition to adding new enemies, dungeons, and adventures, it had raised the level maximum to give the heroes more room to grow. The level maximum had been raised several times since then, until it had reached the current level 90. The last increase had been part of the *Sacred Heart* expansion pack released three years ago. There'd been an announcement that, with the *Homesteading the Noosphere* expansion pack, the level maximum would rise to 100.

That meant many players had plenty of time to level up their Adventurer alter egos. It wasn't at all surprising that, right now, just before the release of the new expansion pack, about half the players had hit the level maximum.

"......I'm not so sure about that."

"Why not?"

In spite of the circumstances, Naotsugu didn't seem discouraged. Shiroe envied his optimism. He didn't have that particular type of resilience.

What he did have right now was a vague uneasiness. As if spurred on by that unease, he mentally began pulling words together.

"I don't know whether this is some other world or the world in the game, but either way... Just the fact that we've been pulled into it is weird."

"Huh? Well...yeah. What about it?"

"I was just thinking. If things were normal, it wouldn't have been possible for us to wander into another world, but we did. Since something impossible has happened already, we can't trust the normal things to behave the way they usually do. In that case, if we believe we'll be able to survive the way we could under normal circumstances, we'll probably get hurt."

At Shiroe's words, Naotsugu looked taken aback for a moment. Then he pulled a very unpleasant face. "That's one ugly syllogism."

"Still...I think we need to face facts."

"Yeah, but…"

Naotsugu flexed his hand, opening and clenching his fist, as if uncertain about whether or not it was safe to trust his supposedly level-90 body.

"One other thing. Since all this has been going on, I'd forgotten about it, but they've probably introduced that new expansion pack by now."

"*Homesteading the Noosphere*? That one?"

"Right. If we assume the new expansion pack has been installed, then there'll be new zones, plus new items, monsters, and quests. They may even have redesigned existing zones."

"Now that you mention it…I guess so."

Shiroe had looked away from Naotsugu, but the words kept coming. "It looks as though I can use spells without any trouble, but if I use them straight from the spell book, I have to select them from the menu first. That's slow, so it would be dangerous in the middle of a fight. I checked, and if I register shortcuts, I just have to say a short chant to use them."

"Yeah. I know what you're talking about; I checked to see if I could use the sword techniques I've got registered a little while back."

"That doesn't mean we'll be able to win a battle, though."

"It doesn't?"

"About how tall are you, Naotsugu? In real life, I mean."

"A hundred and eighty-three. Same as my character."

Naotsugu waved one hand, skimming it over the top of his head.

"I see. I guess it wouldn't feel that weird for you, then. My height's a few centimeters off, and it feels pretty strange. It feels…a bit like I'm wearing shoes with really thick soles, I guess. If the lengths of your legs and arms are different, it makes things feel weirder, I think. There's a gap between these bodies and our real ones. In other words, these bodies aren't the ones we're used to. Even if we can use sword skills and spells, if things feel this odd, I don't know how well we'll be able to move in an actual fight."

"Oh. Yeah, there's that. Trouble city. Pain in the butt."

"…And on top of that, under the circumstances, it won't be easy to keep an eye on our statuses." Naotsugu looked puzzled, so Shiroe explained.

"It's true that if we concentrate on our foreheads, we can see the status screen. If we form a party, we should be able to check each other's HP, but it's not going to be easy to keep a close eye on our statuses when we're fighting. I might be able to manage, but you're usually out on the front line facing down enemies. It's going to be hard to pay attention to status when you're out there trading blows."

"So battles will be pretty tough?"

"It's probably safer to assume so."

Although Shiroe didn't bring it up, their vision would pose a big problem, too. When playing the game on a computer, it was possible to pull back and view the situation from a wider perspective. Under the circumstances, though, they'd only be able to see the 120 degrees directly in front of them.

When they fought trolls, hill giants, or other huge enemies, they'd be dealing with blind spots unlike anything they'd had to field before. Battles would pose a mountain of problems.

"Is that all?"

"...Not quite."

"Well, what is it? Is it hard to talk about or something?"

Shiroe was startled by the sound of his own troubled sigh. To be honest, all the issues he'd spoken about before—problems with battles, differences between their current situation and the game—were trivial. They'd be tough to deal with, certainly, and they'd make battles more difficult, but he didn't think any of them would be impossible to overcome. He'd detoured onto those topics to buy himself time, because the subject still to be broached was an unpleasant one.

"C'mon, Master Counselor. The suspense is killing me. Speak."

Naotsugu always called him that, but Shiroe didn't feel cut out to be a counselor. He was talking about all sorts of things now, but only because he was talking to Naotsugu. Ordinarily, Shiroe was far more likely to worry about this and that on his own privately. The Debauchery Tea Party had nicknamed him "the Counselor" because he tended to take all the details into consideration, and since he was good at talking, they'd handed him the roles of negotiator and strategist. That was all.

"—There are about 1.2 million characters registered on the Japanese *Elder Tales* server and about 100,000 active users."

"Yeah? Yeah, that sounds about right."

Just about everyone who played *Elder Tales* was familiar with that number.

"Since they released the expansion pack today, I assume more players were logged in than usual. I'd estimate that there were about thirty thousand users on the Japanese server. From the percentage of people on my friend list that are logged in, that's probably a fairly accurate guess. If that's true, it's safe to assume that about thirty thousand Japanese users got dragged into this other world, and we still don't know what's going on with the American, European, or Chinese servers."

Naotsugu nodded.

"In other words, there are at least thirty thousand people here—"

Shiroe intentionally avoided saying *gamers*.

"—but no government and no laws."

▶ 3

Afterward, Naotsugu and Shiroe decided to go into town together. They'd tried to talk things through, but there was no getting around the fact that they had a fundamental lack of information. Right now, they needed all the information they could get. What had passed as common knowledge when they were just playing *Elder Tales* might not be true anymore.

Just to be on the safe side, Naotsugu and Shiroe formed a party. Parties were one of the *Elder Tales* communication functions: Teams formed to do battle together. Unlike guilds, they were temporary associations. As a party, they'd be able to check each other's HP and see whether or not the other's status was abnormal; if they were in the same zone, they could tell how far away the other was and in which direction.

*   *   *

The town of Akiba was a noncombat zone. The instant a player tried to do battle in Akiba—whether they were fighting another player or a non-player character—all the guards in the town would converge on them, and they'd be teleported straight into jail. If a player attacked a guard, they would be considered guilty of rebellion against the security forces and destroyed on the spot.

There were lots of characters in *Elder Tales* who weren't players, such as the people who lived in the towns. The game system referred to them as non-player characters, but in the game itself, they were called People of the Earth. Most of them were either shopkeepers who sold a variety of wares or personnel in charge of guild registries and other service facilities, and if you talked to them, they'd give you information or quests to perform.

Since some of the formidable guards were over level 100, no player stood a chance in a fight against them. The town was also an area where monsters never appeared, so when *Elder Tales* was just a game, Akiba had been considered one of the safest zones in the world.

Outside the abandoned building, a wind like the beginning of summer—warm with a slight edge of moisture—was blowing across the town. There was the smell of damp earth, and the leaves and grasses rustled faintly as the wind stirred them. It all seemed so natural that Shiroe felt his awareness that this was a game begin to evaporate. The world his five senses showed him was overwhelmingly real, and the feeling that this was another world grew stronger while the idea that it might be virtual reality faded.

Rounding a bend in the alley, they emerged onto a wide four-lane road. On the corner, a smart building made of composite materials stood like a monolith. Akiba's main intersection. Beyond it, the plaza in front of the train station. Every structure was either covered in vines or had already toppled and ceded its place to huge, ancient trees.

The place felt nothing like the high-tech, steel-and-glass Akihabara of the real world. The colorful signs and gaudy light-up decorations were broken, leaning drunkenly or snapped in two, and the buildings were supported by enormous ginkgoes and elms that had grown up right beside them.

The roads had nearly vanished under the soil, and while traces of asphalt could still be seen on the main streets, the backstreets were covered in damp earth, leaf mold, and jade-green moss, like trails in a nature park. A hybrid car, abandoned aeons ago, had rusted out, become overgrown with weeds, and now provided shelter for small animals.

Still, even in this pitiful state, Akiba was beautiful. It wasn't a polished, stylized beauty, but the buildings were surrounded by all the shades of green there were, and even as ruins, they seemed full of life. Players and non-player characters had staked claims to the mixed-use buildings and moved in, and the temporary shops and stalls they'd set up lined the streets like stands at a bazaar in a warm southern country. This was Shiroe's hometown, the Akiba he knew from *Elder Tales*, in the flesh.

Under ordinary circumstances in *Elder Tales*, the plaza in front of the station would have been an incredibly lively place, filled with players who were setting up stalls to sell their items to other players or killing time while they waited for companions to arrive so that they could leave for a quest or a battle.

Now, though, the atmosphere in the plaza was one of bewilderment, confusion, and muddled irritation. Even a quick glance showed that several hundred players had gathered there. Shiroe sensed eyes watching him from the ruined buildings that overlooked the plaza, from several narrow alleys—even from the elevated railroad tracks that had collapsed and were beyond use.

They'd probably gravitated here looking for help of some sort. Maybe they were hoping one of the administrators would suddenly appear in the plaza, give them a rundown of what had happened, and say, "That concludes the event. What did you think? Wasn't it fantastic?"

Even the players who were clinging to that fragile hope seemed afraid to talk openly with people they didn't know. Even here, out in the plaza, conversations were far more hushed than usual. The majority of the crowd was clustered in small groups here and there, casting wary glances at the people around them. Once in a while there was a sob or a yell from someone who'd reached their limit.

Although they might not have been consciously aware of it, everyone seemed to have realized that, under the circumstances, there was no telling what might happen. However, even then, no one was trying to do anything constructive, a fact that vaguely irritated Shiroe.

How long are these guys planning to just sit here doing nothing? Are they for real? ...Whoa. Shiroe flinched and glanced away. *He caught me looking.*

The player's eyes had seemed to be pleading for something, radiating misery. Shiroe didn't consider himself all that delicate, but he certainly didn't like having someone stare a hole in him with dull, leaden eyes.

...And besides. *It's irritating.* The player crouched there, pleading. Complaining without trying to do a thing for himself. Not that he'd expected otherwise, but having several hundred players here like this—shoulders limp, heads drooping—was bound to be bad for mental health.

Shiroe himself was only able to do what he was doing because he'd gotten through the first rush of anguish before he had time to really feel it and because talking with Naotsugu had calmed him down. He was well aware that there wasn't that much of a difference between him and the players who were just sitting here waiting for help.

That knowledge only amplified the irritation. .

"Shiroe? Shiro, kiddo!" The voice belonged to a woman. Her call hadn't been all that loud, but in the sunken, gloomy mood of the crowded square, her bright, bell-like voice stood out sharply. Shiroe whipped around as if he'd been stung, searching for the voice's owner.

"Mari, Mari. Not so loud. Y-y-you'll stand out."
Shiroe tugged at Marielle's arm.

"Standin' out can't be worse than blendin' in with all these funeral goers."

Marielle—a female player nicknamed Mari—kept talking, paying no heed to Shiroe.

"Perfect timin'. I was lookin' for you, kiddo."

"...You were? Um. Why?"

"Whoa. Check out the babe. Shiro, where've you been hiding this one, you panties perv?!"

"Naotsugu, forget the panties for now, all right?"

They were headed away from the plaza toward an alley where they'd be a bit more sheltered from prying eyes. Not that they were planning to do anything shady; it was just hard to stomach the atmosphere in the plaza. Add the fact that Marielle was even more well-known than Shiroe, and being careful of their surroundings seemed like a good idea.

"Draggin' me into an alley like this... You're growin' up, kiddo."

"I have no intention whatsoever of doing anything like that."

"...Aw. You got yourself a girlfriend, huh? Sniffle, sob."

"That's not it, either. Look, I'm sorry, okay? I'm sorry. Oh, and this is Naotsugu."

"This is definitely Naotsugu. I'm Shiroe's friend... And you, miss?"

"I'm Marielle. Call me Mari or Sis. Wow! Naotsugu, hon, you sure look sharp! Are you two a stage act?"

Marielle was giggling. Shiroe gave her a hard look, trying to figure out what she'd actually meant, but he couldn't see anything like malice in her beaming face. He was forced to conclude that she'd been serious, which left him with absolutely no idea how to respond.

Marielle, who even in this ghastly situation was somehow managing to turn her smile on both of them, was a Cleric. There were twelve classes in *Elder Tales*, and all players had to choose one before starting on their adventures. Cleric was one of the three Recovery classes, and it had the greatest curative powers.

Healers had high survival abilities but low attack power. They were in their element when adventuring with a party, and conversely, they weren't good at acting alone. Since the principle of the Recovery classes was to help others, they tended to attract shy, quiet people. Marielle was the exception to the rule.

A white healer's robe and long, wavy green hair. Elves tended to have attractive, regular features; this had been true before, too, when *Elder Tales* was a game. Of course, in the game world, everyone was good-looking, but even then, for some reason, certain men and women were more popular with other players than most. *Elder Tales*'s voice chat function had made this even more apparent than normal, and Marielle's cheery Kansai dialect and her eagerness to help out had made her a widely recognized player. Her popularity was based on her unreserved candidness, and it was closer to that of a school idol than a girl who attracted guys right and left.

Marielle had no feminine clinginess about her, and both guys and girls adored her. Unlike Shiroe, who had acquired his many acquaintances as a natural consequence of his long gaming career, Mari was good at looking out for people and had lots of friends in the truest sense of the word. As the leader of the Crescent Moon League guild, she looked after several dozen companions, and since she was constantly holding feasts in the taverns of Akiba, she had a reputation as one of the best sources of information in *Elder Tales*.

"You look like you've been thinkin' too hard about mean stuff, kiddo."

"...Well, um..."

Shiroe wondered a bit uneasily whether his face really did look that sour. Under the circumstances, expressions were bound to be rather grim, but he was more worried about the phenomenon he'd noticed after the incident occurred: the one where physical characteristics from the real world were reflected in this one.

In the real world, people said Shiroe had mean eyes, and he had a bit of a complex about that. It was one of the reasons he was still waffling about making the switch from glasses to contacts. He was afraid it would make his eyes seem even more hostile.

Now that *Elder Tales* had become another reality, being told that he looked like he'd been "thinkin' too hard about mean stuff" flustered him. It made him feel as though people had found out about his real-life mean eyes.

But even Mari doesn't look quite...

He snuck a glance at Marielle, looking for changes. Her face clearly wasn't a typical forest elf's face.

"Well, I do sympathize. Even I feel like looking gloomy. Today's been much too much, if you ask me. I think I might go bonkers if I quit jokin' around."

Bright hazel eyes. Her elfin face, which should have looked aristocratic, now had eyebrows that were a bit on the thick side and a smiling mouth that was a little too big. Even that was enough to make it seem warm, friendly, and much more like Marielle. Shiroe had never met Marielle in person, but he could tell with startling clarity that this was her.

"What's with that look, hm? …Aha. You're thinkin', *But she's always like this*, aren'tcha!"

Marielle poked Shiroe's forehead with a finger.

"Normally, I joke around because I like it. What I'm doin' now is active escapism. This is just insane, y'know. I have no idea what to do."

"Shiro. Is this lady always like this?"

"Mm-hm. Always. Exactly like this."

"…And this is what she's like when she's faking it."

"Apparently. I can't tell the difference, either."

Naotsugu had been caught off guard by Marielle's words, but he seemed to have slowly come to grips with the idea that this was just who she was. Noticing his discomfort, Marielle laughed. When Shiroe and Naotsugu looked at her, though, her laugh faltered. She gave a small sigh.

"…Well. Right… This really does beat all, doesn't it?"

"Yes, it does. Should we trade information?"

"Probably we should. Now, where to start…? Ah, no, wait. It's better to be careful, isn't it? Let's go back to my place. You okay with that, Naotsugu?"

Marielle was inviting them back to her guildhall. Agreeing that it would be easier to relax once they were there, the three detoured around Fleig's Tavern and made for the guild center.

Every town had guild centers. In many cases, they were big multipurpose buildings, which housed several different facilities, and in Akiba, the building itself was set up as a zone. Several non-player characters were busily working away in the entry hall. They were guildhall employees, and they could carry out the procedures for establishing a guild if spoken to. They were also tasked with registering nonaffiliated players to guilds and with handling the paperwork for players leaving their guilds.

The building held a bank branch as well. All players had accounts at this in-game bank, which could be used to store money and valuables. Renting out guildhalls was another important role the guild center played. Guildhalls were independent midsized zones, with combined office and living spaces that ranged in size from three to ten rooms.

In *Elder Tales*, some zones were available for purchase and could be bought by individual players. Since anyone who purchased a zone could change the settings for that zone—restricting access so that only specified players were allowed to enter or leave, for example—many players bought small or midsized zones to use as residences. Although it was called "purchasing," any player who wanted to buy a zone had to pay an additional one–five hundredth of the initial lump sum every month as a maintenance fee. For that reason, it wasn't a practical proposition for any player who wasn't fairly well off.

The concept behind guildhalls was similar: They were dedicated zones that could be purchased by guilds, and it was standard for guilds that were above a certain size to have a guildhall in the guild center. These halls could be used to store trophies and materials won in monster battles and items manufactured by the guild and as a meeting place for guild members.

No exception to the rule, the Crescent Moon League had a space in the guild center.

Shiroe and Naotsugu went up a wide staircase to the guild center's second floor. After registering as guests in front of a big set of double doors, they entered the Crescent Moon League's guildhall.

Inside, the guildhall had the standard shabby-office look of all the rented guildhalls in the Akiba guild center. Technically, it was only the flooring and wallpaper that made them seem "standard." Players who purchased or rented zones were free to decorate them any way they liked. The members of the Crescent Moon League kept their guildhall spick-and-span, and they'd refurbished it to make it more comfortable. The walls had wood paneling added, and it gave the place a warm, homey feel.

"See? We won't be bothered here," Marielle said and led them deeper into the guild.

▶ 4

"C'mon in. Go ahead, sit anywhere. You, too, hon. Just pick a spot."

In a room deep inside the guildhall, Marielle threw herself onto a sofa that was buried in fluffy pink cushions and gestured for Shiroe and Naotsugu to sit.

"This is a pretty estrogen-heavy room."

"Sure is. After all, I'm the guild master. The leader's room should exude the leader's dignity."

Pink cushions. Teddy bears. A canopy bed. A tapestry with a picture of an enormous dog with its chest puffed out in a self-important way. Curtains edged with beige lace. The room looked pretty undignified to Shiroe, and he was finding it hard to relax. The room would have been nothing if he'd seen it on a game screen, but now that he was actually inside, the atmosphere was overpowering.

Part of what made it so uncomfortable was that it felt like someone else's personal space. The fact that it belonged to free and easy Marielle softened the edges a bit, but if this had been a lady's private room, he would have been getting ready to beat a retreat.

This was Shiroe's first visit to the guildhall, but he thought the place was probably pretty expensive. This whole room—which, although a bit too frilly, was fairly spacious—was reserved for the guild master's use, and the hall held another five or six workrooms and storage rooms.

I'd say... forty thousand gold coins for the initial cost and eighty for the monthly maintenance fee, he estimated.

"How do things look on your end, Mari?"

Marielle must have checked ahead of time because she answered without hesitation.

"There were nineteen of us online, includin' yours truly. Eighteen of us are in Akiba. They're all feelin' a bit lost and lonesome, so most of 'em are here at the hall... Oh, don't worry. They won't hear us unless we start yellin'."

Eighteen in Akiba... Did that mean the last member was in another zone? When Shiroe asked, it turned out that the last member had just happened to be away and was currently in another city.

"From what I hear, things look about the same in Shibuya, Minami, Susukino, and Nakasu."

That meant all five major cities on the Japanese server had been affected. Marielle had probably checked in with her wide network of friends using the telechat function.

"Hey, don't tell me the gates aren't—"

"Afraid so," Marielle answered Naotsugu. "The intercity transport gates aren't workin'... We're all cut off from each other."

That was new information.

Akiba, Shibuya, Minami, Susukino, and Nakasu were the five main player cities on the Japanese server. There were several other towns— towns with shops inhabited by non-player characters—but the services in these five cities were the most complete by far.

The five cities had been added with various expansion packs and had been designed to act as starting points for beginning players. This meant that all the players on the Japanese server had chosen one of these five cities as their hometown and base of operations. Each of the cities held a transport gate that linked it to the others, allowing players to travel instantaneously from one city to another... But now these gates weren't functioning.

"So we could maybe get to Shibuya, but it'll be pretty tough to get to the other cities."

"Well, and even Shibuya's... How far is it again? I think you'd have to cross seven or eight zones to get there."

"Four at best," Shiroe said absently.

If the gates between the cities weren't working, it was a big problem.

In *Elder Tales*, a game designed to look like a medieval fantasy, the main modes of transportation for Adventurers were walking or horseback. However, in this half-sized virtual Earth, home of the Half-Gaia Project, traveling that way would take far too long. For that reason, players had been provided with Fairy Rings and the transport gates that linked the cities.

The gates had been placed only in player cities. They were teleportation-style devices designed to allow travel between cities with almost no time spent in transit. If those gates were off-line, it would be much, much harder to reach distant cities.

For example, Susukino was located where Sapporo would be on a map of the real Japan. Anyone who wanted to go there from Akiba (Tokyo) would have to cross a vast number of zones. Even in the game, it would probably take more than a week. Of course, that would be a week in game time, but under the circumstances, game time was the only time there was.

"Say, kiddo. Any idea how things got this way?"

Shiroe and Naotsugu were silent. They had no answers, but at the sight of Marielle's slightly discouraged face, Shiroe wished he'd been able to tell her something. As things stood, it was a question he simply didn't have the strength to answer.

"…It's all right, miss. Cheer up. Things are obviously pretty bad, but they're not half as bad as they could be."

"Are you sure about that?"

Marielle sounded dejected.

Naotsugu kept going, speaking firmly in an attempt to cheer her up.

"Maybe we've gotten pulled into some other world, but there must be several thousand Japanese in here, y'know? If people from the other servers are here, too, that's several hundred thousand of us. With that many people in the same boat, it's nowhere near as bad as it could be. We all speak the same language, and we've got some assets on hand. I mean, look, we've just gotten exiled, and we're able to be here, with a roof over our heads, talking. We haven't checked into this yet, but we think we might be as strong as our characters, and we can probably use magic and sword skills. In other words, we've already got the minimum of what it's going to take to survive here. Compared to the fantasy standards like being marooned in another world or getting exiled to another dimension, we've got it pretty good. Talk about an easy win."

"You know a lot about stories like that, Naotsugu?"

"Yeah, I'd say I do. I read all sorts of stuff when I was a kid."

Even as he asked that pointless question, Shiroe felt his respect for Naotsugu grow. He was right. Shiroe seemed to have fallen into the habit of seeing the glass as half-empty, and it had left him unable to see the bright side of things.

"I see… Wow. You're so right!"

Marielle seemed to feel the same way as Shiroe. She looked at Naotsugu, her face flooded with gratitude, and suddenly grabbed him and pulled him to her.

"Yes! Well said! That was impressive, hon! I'm real touched! You're a lifesaver!"

"Whoa— Wha?! Wh-wh-what's with this lady?!"

Pressed to Marielle's ample bosom, Naotsugu struggled, flustered, but Marielle only hugged him harder, shaking him like a puppy with a toy.

"Mari? Do we have guests?"

A woman knocked and entered. She wore glasses, and when she saw Marielle and Naotsugu, she looked terribly embarrassed.

"Hello, Miss Henrietta. We're intruding."

"Not in the least, Master Shiroe. It's good to see you. Shall I come back later?"

"I'd rather you stopped her, actually."

"Yes, absolutely. —Mari, that's *enough*! Would you think before you do things like that?!"

Henrietta, the woman who'd entered the room at Shiroe's request, was in charge of the guild's accounts. She grabbed Marielle's shoulders and pulled her away, scolding loudly.

"Whoa! Henrietta? Listen, I just heard somethin' fantastic. This sweetheart here said the most amazin' thing! Absolutely wonderful!"

"That is *not* what we're talking about now! I can't believe you! At a time like this! Think about the situation!!"

Shiroe chuckled a little, both at the sight of Naotsugu—who was limp and red-faced—and at Marielle and Henrietta.

Henrietta was one of the Crescent Moon League's executive members, and she and Shiroe had met before. She was a Bard, in charge of the guild's accounts, and a terribly competent individual. Since she wore glasses, too, Shiroe had always felt a secret kinship with her. Now, on seeing the other-world version of Henrietta, he realized that sense of kinship had been all in his head.

Henrietta's wavy, honey-colored hair framed an oval face, and although both her features and her light brown eyes were sharp, she was quite beautiful. Not only that, but it was the beauty of a capable secretary. There was something a bit librarian-esque about her clothes; they accented her graceful, mature beauty and suited her very well.

It seemed a little like blasphemy for a game-crazy college student like Shiroe to even look her in the eye.

Since Henrietta had joined them, they reviewed their conversation up to the point where she'd come in and briefly reported their individual circumstances—that said, it had been only half a day since they'd found themselves in this world, and none of their reports revealed any new information.

"So… What should we do?"

"For now, I think we'd do best to stay in close contact with the rest of the group and concentrate on avoiding confusion," Henrietta said.

It was a very levelheaded decision, and Shiroe agreed. Unless they avoided thinking about the distant future and concentrated on doing what they could right now, he felt as if they'd go under.

"They're right, Mari. Both Master Shiroe and Master Naotsugu are entirely correct. Fortunately, we have the guildhall, and I think we should all… Yes, I know it will be a bit cramped, but it would be best if the whole group slept here."

"True."

Henrietta and Marielle's discussion seemed to make Naotsugu break out in a cold sweat.

"What's the matter, Naotsugu?" Shiroe murmured.

"Nothing!" Naotsugu said in hasty denial. "It's just way too sudden, that's all." Although he was always tossing around risqué comments, apparently even he wasn't good at handling direct attacks.

"What's wrong, hon? Don'tcha like boobies? Wanna touch?"

At Marielle's cheery words, Naotsugu quickly averted his eyes. Probably because he was indeed a guy, he did keep sneaking glances anyway.

Well, Mari's gorgeous, and she has an excellent figure, Shiroe thought. *I can sympathize.*

Marielle had put Shiroe through this, too, back when they'd first met. Of course, Shiroe had held out obstinately—"…Yes? What are these fatty growths? They're heavy. Get them out of my face"—all the way to the end. Ego, once again.

Back then, of course, *Elder Tales* was still just a game. Things like this had been limited to suggestive talk and getting two characters together on-screen, and by now—possibly because she'd grown tired of it—Marielle didn't tease Shiroe much.

"Why is this lady so *open* about this stuff?! It's freaking me out."

"Mari went to an all-girls school. This is how native Osakans turn out if you don't dilute them with something else… Mari?! Things like that were fine when this was a game, but right now, we're in a state of emergency! Control yourself!!"

Marielle took Henrietta's scolding with dejected meekness. The fact that she would let herself be scolded, even though she was the guild master, was one of her good points.

Shiroe wasn't currently part of a guild, and even now he had a vague mistrust of the entire system, but he certainly didn't see all players who belonged to guilds as enemies. He'd hated the guild system, yes, but that was several years ago, and although he still had some doubts about it, by now he'd accepted it for what it was. He'd been in several parties with Marielle and Henrietta, and Marielle had used her wide network of acquaintances to help him out on occasion. Shiroe had a hunch that cheerful busybody Marielle had noticed that he was a coward about relationships and tended to keep his distance from people and that she tried to make things easier for him.

Mari's more of a grown-up than I am. Just like Naotsugu... Well, not exactly like Naotsugu.

Marielle wasn't doing any of it to keep Shiroe in her circle of acquaintances so she could use him or profit by the relationship. She was doing it because that was the sort of person she was and because she couldn't help looking out for people. Shiroe didn't think it was something she did especially for him, either; she probably did similar things for everyone around her.

Although I do wish she wasn't quite so...touchy-feely... Oh. Maybe that's it. She acts a lot like Naotsugu. That could be why she took to him so easily...

It was probable that the members of the Crescent Moon League had gathered simply because they liked Marielle. Leading close to twenty members and being attentive to all of them was a truly monumental responsibility. Marielle was a good-natured, trustworthy player, and so Shiroe thought it was probably best to tell her what he could predict about the situation in as much detail as possible.

While Marielle listened to what Shiroe had to say, she paid extra attention to the things they'd need to keep in mind during battle and asked several astute questions. When he mentioned the number of people who were probably on the server and that there was a good chance that trouble would break out among the players, her face clouded.

"I see… You're right. That's a huge possibility, come to think of it. We might end up dealin' with fraud and harassment, as well as straight-up violence…"

Unlike Shiroe, who only had to look out for himself, Marielle had friends she'd need to take care of. On top of that, she was a woman.

"—Hey, that's right! Listen up, lady! Don't go doing stuff like— Like that thing you just did, without thinking about it. Use your common sense, or go find some. There's nothing good about being featherbrained."

"Ack?! You're so right! I'm heavy boobed but featherbrained! —But I don't see what gives *you* the right to tell me that, seein' as we just met. Mean ol' Naotsugu! Dummy! Dummy!"

"No, Master Naotsugu has an excellent point. I insist you fix that girls'-school habit of hugging people indiscriminately, Mari."

"Aw, who cares?! Nobody, that's who! And anyway, what's this fancy-schmancy Henrietta business, Umeko-in-real-life?!"

"Yeeeeeeeghk! You *promised* you'd never tell!!"

…Apparently Henrietta and Marielle knew each other outside *Elder Tales* as well. Shiroe had been telling them some pretty serious stuff, and wondering how much of it had actually gotten through was giving him a headache.

"Honestly! That's enough time wasted on that foolish girl," Henrietta said pragmatically. "Now, I suppose a prompt resolution is…"

"Probably not in the cards," Shiroe answered. "I don't think we should hold our breath."

"Isn't there anythin' we can do?"

Marielle frowned, knitting her brow. She didn't seem able to accept the idea. Shiroe knew exactly how she felt, and he'd already thought about that particular question. As a result, he'd decided to split up the responsibility of gathering information with Naotsugu, the way they were doing now.

At the moment, they knew very little. However, although gathering information was high on the list of things he and Naotsugu could and should do, it wouldn't necessarily be top priority for everyone. Unlike Shiroe, Marielle was a guild master. Naturally, that meant there were more people she had to protect, but it also meant there was more she could do.

                              *   *   *

Although guilds were common in general, there were all sorts of different styles. Differences in activities, goals, and scale resulted in a huge variety of orientations. In terms of activities, the most common type of guild was the fighting guild. These were guilds formed to provide backup in battles—one of the highlights of *Elder Tales*—and the focus of member activities was battling in open-air and dungeon zones. The guild's role was to make it easy to find people to fight alongside you that day, otherwise known as party members. It was easier to recruit people you already knew, and it often made team plays go more smoothly.

As the biggest player city on the Japanese server, Akiba boasted a large population. Its most famous fighting guilds were the Knights of the Black Sword, Honesty, D.D.D., and the West Wind Brigade.

Another type of guild was the production guild. In addition to the main classes, which determined players' fighting styles, *Elder Tales* offered various subclasses. Players who belonged to production-type subclasses and used their skills to create items were known as "artisans." The levels for main classes and subclasses were independent of each other, and although it was possible to level up both at the same time, some players preferred to spend their time quietly in town, using their subclass skills to play at being merchants. Players like these joined production guilds. Such guilds tended to be large, since the things players expected of them—bulk purchase of materials and warehouse storage—could be performed to better advantage if there were lots of people involved. The most famous production guilds in Akiba were probably the Marine Organization and the Roderick Trading Company.

Marielle's Crescent Moon League was a small adventure support guild. Adventure support guilds provided assistance for battles, production, or whatever their members wanted to do. Since they didn't specialize either way, their members didn't benefit quite as much. However, they compensated for this shortcoming with a relaxed, homey atmosphere, and in fact, most small and midsized guilds tended to be adventure support guilds.

The Crescent Moon League was a relatively well-known example. It lacked the name recognition and clout of the big fighting guilds, and it couldn't match the revenue or scale of the big production guilds, but it had an established reputation for support for midlevel Adventurers and for being light on its feet.

"For now, I think protecting yourselves should be your first priority."

"What he said. From what I saw, there are a lot of girls in this guild, right?"

Henrietta nodded in response to Shiroe's and Naotsugu's comments. Although the town was a noncombat zone, under the circumstances, there was no telling what might happen… And that was assuming the noncombat settings were still in place. Until they managed to check, they had no guarantee that that was the case.

We'll have to find some way to look into that later.

Shiroe made a mental note.

"Next, I think you should temporarily pull your items from the market."

"Huh? The market? And why's that?"

"Ah… Yes, you're right."

Markets were a service provided in all major cities by specific non-player characters. Players were able to sell off their items at will by giving them to these non-player characters and setting a price. Although there were many ways for players to do business with other players, the market was an extremely simple, handy way to sell off surplus items and items players had made.

"The Crescent Moon guild has quite a lot of raw material, doesn't it? I'd assume many of your members have put items on the market privately, too. In a situation like this, prices can change drastically, even for old items. They may have acquired new effects, or someone may find a brand-new way to use them. If you have some money on hand, I'd pull back for a while and keep an eye on market conditions."

"Okay. Roger that. You're right."

"Then, too, we won't be able to check the Internet anymore."

Marielle and Henrietta nodded meekly.

When *Elder Tales* was just a game, Shiroe and the others had played it while seated in front of monitors. That meant they'd been able to casually surf the Internet while they played, and most players had. *Elder Tales* was an enormous, unbelievably complex game. Because no one player could ever know everything there was to know about that world, solution sites had been players' constant salvation.

Maps and characteristics of all sorts of zones. The routes that connected them. The monsters and items that appeared there. Where players had to go to find non-player characters and what types of non-player characters they'd be. Having all this information in front of them as they played the game had been the most common way to play *Elder Tales*.

Of course even solution sites were far from all-powerful. Still, they often discussed popular areas and places where players could earn money efficiently.

They also listed dangerous places that players would do well to avoid.

"It's weird for me to say this since we came to trade information, but information is going to be one of the most valuable things we have from now on. You remember there's a new expansion pack, don't you?"

"*Homesteading the Noosphere*? Yep."

"That's the one. We'll need information, not just on the new zones the expansion pack added, but on zones and towns that were already here. We can't check solution sites if we get bogged down now."

"True…"

And so, after that, the four of them drew a schematic diagram of the zones around Akiba based on the information they remembered.

Although the Japanese server held tens of thousands of zones, that figure included single inn rooms, small abandoned buildings, and private zones like the guildhall that were rented out to players. There were far fewer field zones (forests, hill country, ghost towns, ruins, and other outdoor areas) and dungeon zones (the insides of old subway tunnels and gigantic structures). "Fewer" was a relative term, of course: There were several thousand at least, and even Shiroe couldn't claim to have a sufficient grasp of all of them. However, he did have eight years of gaming under his belt, and he knew his way around the world of *Elder Tales* much better than most players. Naotsugu had been out of action for a while, but he knew quite a lot about the older zones. Marielle and Henrietta also checked their memories against each other, and the end result, while terribly incomplete, was a zone schematic.

They'd filled in quite a lot of zones on the map, drawn lines to show the connections between them, and written in several hundred names with a focus on the field zones they visited frequently. There was no telling whether they'd still have to investigate each of these places one by one, but even this sketchy map was better than nothing at all.

"Thanks a bunch, kiddo. You, too, Naotsugu."

"It's the least we could do. We're already imposing on you."

"Yeah, and it's not like we did much anyway."

"No, it's a big help. I know Shiroe's a good kid."

Marielle sent Shiroe a smile like a sunflower in full bloom.

Mari has the greatest smile. Even when she's tired, even when she's irritated—I really should try to learn from that.

"I couldn't possibly leave you to fend for yourself, Mari."

Shiroe had done his very best, but as usual, he'd missed the mark.

"Wha…?! Now even *you're* sayin' it! Oh, that is *it*. It's curtains for me. I'm pinned as the featherbrained, dumb-broad character for sure. What'll I do, Henrietta?!"

"Why not concentrate on sex appeal?"

Shiroe hastily averted his eyes.

"Wanna touch my boobs? Cop a feel?"

Having been turned down flat by Shiroe, Marielle tried her luck on Naotsugu, who was sitting next to him. Wordlessly, Naotsugu smacked her on the head.

"D-did you just *hit* me?!"

Shiroe assumed Marielle probably used suggestive lines as a way to hide her embarrassment, but now that he was thinking about it, he realized it might explain Naotsugu's off-color comments as well. Seeing Naotsugu respond this way was funny.

"Don't you *ever* learn, you panties woman?!"

"Don't say 'panties'! What's wrong with you anyway, hon?! Are my boobs really that bad?! Are you treatin' me like some old lady?!"

"You make no sense. What's this 'old lady' business? We're pretty much the same age, right?"

Naotsugu whispered his birth date to Henrietta who nodded.

"Mari's three years older."

"There, y'see? I'm *old*! …I'm bad inventory. That must be why Naotsugu's gone to the bad. Just look at him! He defies me, he treats my poor boobs like they're wrinkly old puddin'…"

On the sofa, Marielle whined, kicking her legs like a little kid throwing a tantrum.

In a way, it's really impressive that she can care about stuff like that at a time like this.

Mildly appalled, Shiroe thought that Marielle was the only one who'd be able to expend this much energy over *anything* on the first day of their exile in another world. However, unexpectedly, Naotsugu kept lightly patting Marielle's head as she fussed. He looked as if he was trying to comfort a large dog, but gradually, Marielle did calm down.

"…In any case. I should be going. I've already taken up a lot of your time… I'll go see what else I can learn about the situation."

Shiroe stood, giving a slight bow to Marielle, who was still inclined to sulk, and the sober Henrietta.

"Yeah. I'll go with you… 'Scuse us, ladies!"

It had been more than half a day since the disaster. Some enterprising soul might have fought a monster or two by now. When Shiroe and Naotsugu said their good-byes to the two on the sofa, Henrietta said politely, "I'm sorry we weren't able to show you better hospitality." In contrast, Marielle stood up from the sofa where she'd staged her tantrum, looked Shiroe and Naotsugu square in the eyes, and made a proposition.

"Listen, kiddo. You, too, hon. So, um… It's probably gonna sound like I'm tryin' to take advantage of the situation by askin' this now, but… Would you two join up? Join the Crescent Moon League, I mean."

Her voice held a very uncharacteristic hesitation.

"Well, and look, I know. I'm well aware that you don't feel at home in guilds, kiddo. —Everythin's different now, though. I don't think joinin' up would be a bad idea. You, too, Naotsugu. From what I can see, you haven't signed on with anybody yet… What about it?"

Her troubled expression shifted into one of persuasion. Her voice betrayed no intention of using Shiroe and Naotsugu or of trying to strengthen her own guild. There was nothing in it but simple, unaffected kindness.

However she'd taken Shiroe's silence, it made her wave her hands hastily and continue on.

"We're a pretty laid-back guild. We won't tie you down. We won't do anythin' you wouldn't like, kiddo. You've been through a few dungeons with our younger ones, remember? You know, the Shinjuku subway, Nakano Mall... I don't know why you aren't in a guild, Naotsugu, but the Crescent Moon League is... Well, I think it's a pretty comfortable place myself. What do you say?"

Her green hair swayed across her white healer's robe. To Shiroe, the gentle movement seemed like a visual expression of the consideration she was showing them.

"......"

Wordlessly, Naotsugu looked at Shiroe. The look clearly meant, "It's up to you." *Do we settle down here? Do we stay freelance? It's your call.*

Shiroe wasn't a middle schooler anymore. He could forgive the people who'd used him as a soulless tool all those years ago, and it wasn't that his feelings about it were still muddled and confused. Still, something he couldn't put into words kept him from taking the plunge.

"Mari, I'm sorry. I really can't."

"I see... Okay, then. No help for that."

Marielle's disappointed look lasted only an instant before it was replaced by her usual smile. As always, the smile was bright as a sunflower, and it made Shiroe feel as if he'd been rescued.

If they managed to get back to their world, either through some divine miracle or by sheer coincidence... If Shiroe happened to pass Marielle on the street, he was sure he'd recognize her. The healer's cloak and the luxurious green hair might be nothing more than *Elder Tales* polygon data made real, but Marielle's smile was hers alone. It was nothing anyone could ever imitate.

It certainly wasn't anything a game program could reproduce.

"If you ever need anything, ask us. We'll help."

"Yeah. Any time you need a good Guardian, just yell."

"Will do. Thanks, kiddo. Thanks, hon. You, too: If you need anythin', call me."

Shiroe and Naotsugu waved good-bye, wishing they had Marielle's particular brand of strength.

CHAPTER.
2
SMALL ASSASSIN

► LEVEL: **90**

► RACE: **HUMAN**

► CLASS: **GUARDIAN**

► HP: **13295**

► MP: **6613**

► ITEM 1:

[METEOROS SHIELD]

A MIGHTY SHIELD FORGED
FROM LADINIUM ORE BY
A METEOR STRIKE. THIS
ITEM CAN BE PRODUCED,
BUT YOU'LL NEED THE HELP
OF A PRACTITIONER WHO
CAN SUMMON METEORS.
NAOTSUGU'S SHIELD HAS
PANTIES STICKERS STUCK TO
THE BACK.

► ITEM 2:

[KNIGHT'S CASTLE ARMOR]

HIGH-PERFORMANCE FULL-BODY
ARMOR DROPPED FROM RUSEATO
OF THE SEVENTH PRISON. DUE TO THE
ADDITION OF EXPANSION
PACKS, IT ISN'T STATE-
OF-THE-ART PROTECTIVE
GEAR ANYMORE, BUT IT'S
STILL POWERFUL ENOUGH
FOR LEVEL 90 NAOTSUGU
TO USE.

► ITEM 3:

[PANTIES NOTEBOOK]

A NOTEBOOK USED TO LOG EVIDENCE THAT
ITS BEARER HAS DEFEATED MONSTERS.
IT WAS ORIGINALLY CALLED
"EVIDENCE NOTEBOOK,"
BUT NAOTSUGU
CHANGED THE NAME
WHEN HE REALIZED HE
COULD RENAME ITEMS. THE
NOTEBOOK HAS NO IN-GAME
EFFECT.

<LEATHER SHOES>
USED TO PROTECT YOUR FEET
AND MAKE LONG JOURNEYS
EASIER. EDIBLE IF BOILED.

▶1

—Four days had passed.

Four days since the insanity of being set adrift in another world.

After taking their leave of Marielle, Shiroe and Naotsugu had spent most of their time trekking through the streets of Akiba, gathering information.

Naturally, new facts came to light every day.

The first discovery, and one they'd made quite easily, was that they got hungry. In fact, they'd felt a vague irritation starting at about the time they said good bye to Marielle. However, the tension and fear of the abnormal situation had swamped the irritation, and they'd walked around searching for information until night fell and their legs were like lead without ever realizing that the strange sensation was hunger.

In the end, though, they'd given in to their empty stomachs. At daybreak, Shiroe and Naotsugu bought food at the market and went back to the abandoned building where they'd met the day before. Their attempt at a slightly unhealthy meal (dinner meets breakfast) proved to be a shattering experience.

That morning, Shiroe had purchased roast chicken with orange sauce, a tomato sandwich, chocolate cake, and green tea. Naotsugu had picked up seafood pizza, potatoes and bacon, a Caesar salad, and orangeade. While that may seem extravagant, Shiroe and Naotsugu were both level-90 players with property to match. Besides, everything they'd purchased had been made by artisan players and offered for sale at the market in large quantities. To all appearances, the food was fresh, colorful, and fit for a king.

…But it all tasted exactly the same.

It was, to borrow Naotsugu's disgusted review, like eating soggy, unsalted rice crackers. Shiroe was forced to agree.

As for the beverages, although they were different colors, they both tasted like city tap water.

It didn't taste so bad that they had to spit it out after the first bite. It probably wasn't poison. If they ate enough of it, they felt full, so it was definitely food. But Shiroe and Naotsugu still felt as if the bottom had been kicked out of their morning.

That the taste wasn't terrible enough to provoke instant yelling made it really difficult to deal with. The more they ate, the odder they felt. The insipid flavor seemed to slowly drain the hope out of them. It was a dull, miserable taste.

After buying up several different kinds of food, they learned a few more things. All the foods they were eating had either been made by players or sold by non-player characters. One of the countless sub-classes in *Elder Tales* was Chef. The food items they'd purchased had been created by Chefs using their cooking skills. Because subclasses could be acquired regardless of which of the twelve main classes a player belonged to, it was possible to be a Samurai Chef or a Sorcerer Chef.

Although these Chefs had used their skills to create the food items Shiroe and Naotsugu were eating, cooking in *Elder Tales* was a fairly automatic operation. You approached the kitchen counter object, took the ingredient items out of your pack, and specified which ones to use. Some ingredients could be harvested in various zones, while others— such as meat—could be taken from monsters, and a few could be picked up in dungeons. There were also items like grain, which could be grown by sowing seeds in a field. Non-player characters sold basic ingredients, and it was perfectly possible to purchase ingredients from other players at the market. No matter how a player got the ingredients, all they had to do was select items to view a list of dishes that could be created, then select the dish they wanted to make. In about ten seconds, the ingredients would start to glow, then disappear and be replaced by the finished dish.

Shiroe and Naotsugu had started to wonder whether this push-button preparation method was the problem.

Just yesterday, they'd discovered that unprepared ingredients did taste the way they were supposed to. Oranges, apples, and other fruits were juicy and delicious, and fresh-caught fish smelled like real fish. The salt and sugar they'd bought from non-player characters tasted salty and sweet. Regardless, any dish made by mixing these ingredients together tasted like soggy, unsalted rice crackers.

The phenomenon was inevitable. No matter what they tried, they couldn't change it. On top of that, apparently it wasn't possible to actually cook in this world. When they tried to process an ingredient by hand, it turned into a weird gel-like substance.

With no way around it, Shiroe and Naotsugu bought salt as a stand-alone ingredient along with their other food items and staved off starvation by salting their soggy rice crackers before they ate. It made for a very poor meal, but it was better than having no flavor at all.

Of course what went in had to come out, which meant they discovered that they'd have to go with relative ease as well. Since Shiroe and Naotsugu were guys, this didn't pose much of a problem, provided they didn't mind going outside, although it would have been nice to have toilet paper. Naotsugu muttered, "This must be pretty rough on the girls...," but Shiroe pretended he hadn't heard.

The world held all sorts of things that it did no good for Shiroe to think about. They learned that they needed to sleep, too. Unlike Shiroe's real body, his body in this world was pretty strong. At level 90, even a magic user had corresponding abilities, and stamina seemed to be one of them. However, physical fatigue and the desire for sleep seemed to be two different things, and after being active for a certain amount of time, both Shiroe and Naotsugu would get very sleepy.

When Shiroe and Naotsugu entered an inn, they'd rent a zone for a short period and stay there. Neither of them had ever used this function when *Elder Tales* was a game. When they'd decided to stop playing for a while, all they had to do was find a convenient alley in Akiba and log out. When they played the game, they adventured; when they wanted to rest, they left the game world entirely. Things that they'd taken for granted when they played the game didn't hold true anymore.

Since they kept their bodies while they slept, they needed somewhere relatively safe to put them… And of course, when they woke up, they hadn't returned to the real world.

Speaking of returning to the real world, they'd discovered the answer to another question: Resurrection from death existed even in this version of the *Elder Tales* world. When players died, after a little while they came back to life in the temple in Akiba. If things still worked the way they had in the game, the resurrected player would probably lose a certain amount of experience points or money, but since it hadn't happened to Shiroe or Naotsugu yet, they didn't know for sure.

The fact that resurrection existed meant that death in the game world didn't equal actual extinction. Although that was good news, it also put an end to the hope that death would be a ticket back to the real world.

Death and food. If there was one thing they'd learned from these two basic elements of life, it was that even the most diplomatic speaker couldn't call this world anything but warped and contradictory. At a glance, it seemed to be a faithful real-life reproduction of the *Elder Tales* game world. Shiroe and Naotsugu had acquired their in-game abilities and property and were living in a world that teemed with game monsters. However, the game was a game, not a replica of some other world. Considered as a world with consistent physical laws, this world seemed incredibly incomplete and on the verge of disintegrating to Shiroe.

The biggest example was the food. Roasted fish, which was made by selecting the ingredients salt and fish, didn't taste like either salt or fish. Instead, it turned into something that *looked* exactly like roasted fish but tasted like soggy rice crackers. That said, when they put salt on the roasted fish and ate it, it did taste salty. Sprinkling salt on afterward made it salty, but cooking with salt as an ingredient negated any saltiness.

Just as an experiment, they tried cooking raw fish over a fire and other heat sources, the way it would have been done in the real world. Nothing they tried produced anything they recognized as roasted fish. The end result was always an unidentifiable charred lump.

The same was true of sleeping and going to the bathroom: Neither should be necessary in a game. However, in this real version of *Elder Tales*, Shiroe and Naotsugu did get sleepy, and bathrooms were definitely necessary.

No matter how you looked at it, this world was strange.

Of course, since it actually was a world, there had to be rules behind it somewhere. What they didn't know was whether the world was operating on the *Elder Tales* rules or whether there were different physical rules at play here, completely understandable but belonging to a world that wasn't their own. It almost looked as though *both* ideas were true: two sets of rules mixing in an uncanny way, making the world even more of a chaotic puzzle.

They'd discovered many other things over those four days.

On the second day after the fiasco, Shiroe and Naotsugu screwed up their courage and headed out to one of the field zones. They chose the Forest of Library Towers, a neighboring zone that could be reached by gate from Akiba.

Since the Forest of Library Towers was so close to the starting point, it was a fairly easy zone. Many of the zones around the five major cities were tailored to beginners. In *Elder Tales*, everyone knew that high-level monsters lived deep in the mountains, far from the cities. This was a typical field zone of ruins, haunted by monsters who were somewhere in the level-20 bracket. It was filled with abandoned buildings covered in green vines and parasitic plants, similar to the ones in Akiba.

As its name implied, the Forest of Library Towers was a zone littered with old bookstores, libraries, and laboratories and was connected to several dungeon zones. Although enemies here were weak, they occasionally dropped Esoteric Scrolls as treasures, and the zone was a notoriously profitable hunting ground for newbie Adventurers.

Shiroe and Naotsugu were level-players with plenty of experience points and a good array of equipment, and they'd be tackling weak monsters, none of which would be more than level 25. There was such a huge level difference that they wouldn't get any experience points no matter how many monsters they defeated, but they'd chosen this beginner zone anyway, partly out of caution. In it, they came up against a reality that was harsher than anything they'd imagined.

Battles didn't unfold as planned.

It wasn't that the monsters were tough. All it took to topple a goblin or a gray wolf was a single glancing blow from Naotsugu's sword. Not only that, but a direct hit from one of Shiroe's attack spells would kill a monster, even though, as an Enchanter, his attack spells were the weakest of any magic user's. The level gap was just that big.

However, being able to defeat the enemy didn't mean the battles were easy. The first time he encountered a wolf, and the time he was swarmed by little green goblins brandishing bloodstained, rusty axes, Shiroe was so terrified that his knees would barely hold him. He was breathing ten times faster than he normally did, but even with that much air in his lungs, he felt like he wasn't getting enough oxygen. It was hard to breathe, and his field of vision narrowed. If he hadn't kept telling himself over and over that the enemy's attacks wouldn't do any damage, he might have turned and run.

A little while later, that desperate guess—that they couldn't take damage from these enemies—proved to be correct. At level 90, Shiroe's HP was slightly over eight thousand, and as a Guardian, the class with the strongest Defense, Naotsugu had thirteen thousand. Against them, goblins could only inflict damage in the single digits. Even if the goblins came at them with ferocious shrieks and swung axes down on them with terrible force, it hurt less than taking a punch from an elementary schoolkid. Once they knew for sure that was the case, Shiroe and Naotsugu were finally able to calm down.

Even though they stopped taking any damage once they'd relaxed, the fighting was still hard. Here, too, the weird tension produced by the conflict between natural physical laws and the *Elder Tales* specs reared its head.

In *Elder Tales* battles, once players had formed a party, as Shiroe and Naotsugu had done, they chose team plays and strategies almost unconsciously while keeping an eye on each other's HP via their status screens. Were other enemies approaching while they fought the enemies in front of them? Was the enemy merging or summoning reinforcements? Which enemy should they take down first? Which enemies was it safe to weaken to a certain level and leave for later? These insignificant scraps of information could have a major effect on the outcome of a battle.

Under the circumstances, though, it was hard even to check each other's HP. If they concentrated on their foreheads, the HP display came up in their mind's eye. However, it was incredibly difficult to keep track of numbers and statuses while battling on rubble-strewn, uneven ground. As a magic user, Shiroe had the leeway to watch the whole battlefield from the rear, but Naotsugu had to attract enemy attacks on the front lines and protect the rest of his party, and having lost the wide field of vision and the ability to grasp his surroundings that he'd had in the game, he was practically flying blind.

"This is a lot hairier than I thought it would be."

Naotsugu heaved a deep sigh as they ate the Chinese steamed buns they'd brought for lunch. Since the monsters here were so weak, they were able to fight without worrying about their HP, but how well they'd fare against an opponent on their level was anyone's guess. Dejectedly eating the bland, salted muck that only looked like Chinese steamed buns, Shiroe and Naotsugu compared notes on the battle.

Neither of them had any real-world fighting experience. They had no idea how to get used to the sensations and the fear battles brought, and they weren't sure whether trying to do it this way would actually work. That said, they both knew that if they were scared of puny-level monsters, they'd be in big trouble if anything more serious happened later on. Since *Elder Tales* was a fantasy adventure game, fighting monsters was a major element. Whether this world had been influenced by *Elder Tales* or was the world of *Elder Tales* itself, getting used to fighting was going to be a big prerequisite of survival.

Fortunately, they were both far tougher physically than they'd anticipated. Since they were high-level players, Shiroe's and Naotsugu's bodies didn't seem to get fatigued. Even if they managed to wear themselves out by fighting or traveling, it only took them a few minutes of rest to recharge. They spent nearly all the daylight hours outdoors and used the hours between evening and true night to go to taverns and visit acquaintances in town, looking for new information and talking with players who were in the same situation.

During those first four days, at least on the surface, the town of Akiba remained quiet. The big panic Shiroe had anticipated didn't happen. That might have been because the players had been given the bare minimum required for peace of mind: Food was readily available—even if it tasted abysmal—and they'd seen that death in this world didn't equal extinction. Of course, that didn't mean nothing happened. Several trends began to appear, and while they weren't large, they weren't safe to ignore.

First, the goods offered for sale at the market were rapidly disappearing. Many players seemed to have come to the same conclusion as Shiroe and taken their own items off the market. The remaining items belonged to players who had been lucky enough to not have logged in that day, and as the days went by, even those began to sell out. There were rumors that some of the big artisan guilds were buying up raw materials, and quite a few items became impossible to get. Many players belonged to production classes, but they seemed to have suspended their activities due to the current situation.

Another trend was the guilds' recruiting war and the search for guilds by unaffiliated players. Apparently, humans did feel more at ease when they belonged to something. The disaster seemed to have spurred many unaffiliated players, gamers who'd been content to spend their days carelessly until now, into taking the plunge and joining a guild. If a player was in your field of vision, it was possible to tell their name and which guild they belonged to by checking a menu. However, there was no easy way to see statistics about the whole situation from within the game. For that reason, all Shiroe had to go on was the general ratio of the players he saw, but he felt that the number of unaffiliated players was dwindling.

Of course, as unaffiliated players who were also level 90, Shiroe and Naotsugu were approached by any number of guilds as they wandered through town. Both turned down every single invitation.

Unlike Shiroe, Naotsugu didn't seem to have any particular negative feelings toward guilds. When Shiroe asked him about it, he laughed. "Hanging out with somebody is an end result. You just start running, and you pick up friends along the way. That's how it's usually done."

The Debauchery Tea Party hadn't been a guild, and it hadn't been formed the way guilds were. To Shiroe and Naotsugu, former Tea Party members, a guild was just a name, and names weren't important. In the first place, neither of them had any illusions that belonging to a guild would have protected them from the initial disaster or the resulting chaos.

Unlike Shiroe and Naotsugu, though, many players seemed to feel that the guilds were the only things they could rely on. The twins Shiroe had been with on the day of the disaster seemed to have joined a guild as well. He only saw them once in town, from a distance, but they seemed to be safe, which was a small relief. As if to fulfill unaffiliated players' desire for the reassurance of belonging somewhere, several guilds had launched expansion strategies. Some expanded by recruiting unaffiliated players and swelling their ranks, but it was more common for several small guilds to merge or for big guilds to target and appropriate particular players from other guilds.

Shiroe didn't understand why the guilds would want to boost their numbers. When he asked Marielle, she said it had to do with the current atmosphere in Akiba.

Ever since the disaster, many players seemed to feel that they'd been exiled to this other world. Even Shiroe and Naotsugu felt to some extent that the situation was unfair. However, the irritation the players felt at this unfairness seemed to be much stronger than Shiroe had anticipated. When an entire guild shared this feeling, it turned into active rejection of anything that was not part of that particular guild. In other words, "Everyone who isn't us is the enemy." It was all right to trust members of the same guild, but no one else. In this harsh atmosphere, it could have been a natural attempt at self-defense.

However, that atmosphere had grown too intense, and little by little, friction between the guilds was increasing. Of course, since Akiba was a noncombat zone, there would be no sudden outright attacks. If there were any attempts at starting a fight, at stealing, or at keeping someone prisoner, the guards would immediately teleport in and forcibly arrest the aggressor.

That said, sharp words and harassment didn't necessarily count as "combat." There were all sorts of ways to slip harassment through the gaps in the definition of combat, especially now that players were physically part of this world. Small guilds were often the targets of this sort of harassment. Marielle gave a small smile that was both slightly troubled and intended to gloss over that trouble.

It was while they were talking to Marielle that they uncovered something serious about the zones. Shiroe had absently opened his mental array of icons. Down below the information menu and the guild-related items, he discovered that an unfamiliar item had been added to the list. Although he wasn't used to seeing the item here, he had seen it before. It was the menu that showed the information on the zone he was currently in, and it displayed all the usual items: JAPANESE SERVER / THE TOWN OF AKIBA / URBAN AREA—NO MONSTERS / NON-COMBAT ZONE / ENTRY PERMISSION (UNLIMITED) / EXIT PERMISSION (UNLIMITED).

Shiroe, Marielle, and Naotsugu had been standing and talking in one of Akiba's deserted streets, and so of course the display described Akiba, the zone they were in. No problems there.

The problem was in the next line.

THIS ZONE HAS NO SPECIFIC OWNER AT PRESENT. TO PURCHASE THIS ZONE, YOU'LL NEED SEVEN HUNDRED MILLION GOLD COINS. MONTHLY MAINTENANCE FEES ARE 1.2 MILLION GOLD COINS. PURCHASE? (YES / NO)

That notice was a menu that appeared during purchases of small zones. A smaller abandoned building, for example, or a hotel room or the Crescent Moon League guildhall. Now, although it would take an astronomical sum of money to purchase it, Akiba itself was up for sale.

At first, when Shiroe mentioned it to them, Marielle and Naotsugu laughed. Once they checked their own menus, though, they were struck dumb.

Shiroe had a long history in *Elder Tales*, and he was a high-level player. As players went, he was comparatively wealthy. The total worth of everything in his bank account was about fifty thousand gold coins. He could declare categorically that seven hundred million gold coins wasn't an amount any single player could pay.

However, if one of the major guilds invested all the resources at their disposal—even then, he thought it *probably* wouldn't be possible, but there was no guarantee that it wouldn't be.

If, hypothetically, someone bought the town of Akiba, the purchaser would be able to set entry restrictions. If they didn't like a guild or an individual, they could make the town off-limits to them at the system level.

When Marielle assembled the members of the Crescent Moon League and everyone split up and investigated, they discovered that almost every zone was now for sale. In other words, all zones—urban areas, fields, and dungeons—had been declared ownerless and put up for sale. The only exceptions were places that already had owners, such as the Crescent Moon League guildhall. Zones like that had acquired the option to revert the right of ownership to a deed item.

By the fourth day after the disaster, Shiroe and the others were no longer able to shrug off the major guilds' increasing strength as straightforward expansion strategies.

▶ **2**

On the morning of the fifth day, Shiroe and Naotsugu left their usual inn and headed for the market to buy food for the day. Oddly for him (although it could have been because he'd just woken up), Naotsugu trudged along listlessly.

"What's the matter?"

"...Nnergh. The idea of having to eat that craptastic food for the rest of forever is really bumming me out."

Shiroe knew exactly how Naotsugu felt. He'd never considered himself a gourmet, and he hadn't had brag-worthy eating habits in the real world. Now, though, he realized just how well he'd eaten before.

Those fast-food fried chicken bentos really were tasty. That sixty-eight-yen instant ramen. Mm, and yakisoba bread... All incredible luxuries, come to think of it.

The same went for black tea, coffee, and soft drinks. That every single beverage tasted like city tap water had been really tough to take. From what Shiroe knew, all beverages were made by combining well water with other ingredients. When they'd tried drinking it, just to see, even well water had tasted like city tap water, which meant that the "city tap water" taste was probably all in their heads, and the water was just plain water.

The idea that water mixed with something else was still just water made them feel as if they'd been cheated somehow.

"...That's all there is."

"Well, yeah. I know that. I just think they probably feed you better in jail even. I saw what they served at Abashiri Prison on a TV special one time, and it looked pretty good."

"Yeah."

Come to think of it, it did feel that way. Up until middle school, Shiroe had gone to a public school. The lunches he'd eaten there hadn't been gourmet in any sense of the word, but they'd been far better than this world's universal soggy rice cracker fare.

"So, I've been thinking."

"About...?"

"What if this is some divine torture chamber where we're being forced to eat craptastic food?"

Shiroe was about to tell him that was insane when he realized he had no way to disprove it. It sounded like a far-fetched, nutty idea, but reality was already pretty far-fetched and nutty, and he couldn't just laugh it off as crazy talk.

"If so, that particular god is pretty good at torture."

"That's what I say. What if the food was poison and eating it made you cough up blood, but they kept making you eat it anyway? Doesn't that sound like hell? Like there'd be tormenting demons who force-fed it to you."

You know, that does sound like it could be a Buddhist hell, Shiroe thought.

"It's not like that, though, is it? It's probably some kind of nutritious, and it isn't poison. Even the taste isn't so bad you can't choke it down. For one meal, it'd probably be okay. But it's *the only thing we've got.* There will never, ever be any other flavor. This is all we get, from here to infinity, and we'll just keep getting more and more bummed out— that's some pretty high-level harassment, wouldn't you say?"

"That's why I said they're *good* at torture—not that I don't wish they weren't."

As Shiroe and Naotsugu were talking…

…a pebble bounced off the asphalt at their feet with a faint *click*.

When Shiroe looked up, he saw a tall man standing in the entrance to a crumbling three-story building that had once been some sort of shop.

"That's Akatsuki."

Black hair, black clothes, regular features. The man had a scarf wrapped around his face, hiding his mouth. He nodded to Shiroe.

"Friend of yours?"

"Yeah. This is Akatsuki," Shiroe told Naotsugu as they approached the man. "He's an Assassin."

Shiroe had gotten to know Akatsuki about a year ago. Akatsuki was an extremely taciturn player. This was partly due to the fact that, in this day and age, when practically everyone used voice chat, he preferred old-school text chats. Of course, that only made him a more authentic Assassin. There were quite a few role players like Akatsuki in *Elder Tales*. To Shiroe, role players were players who took atmosphere very seriously.

Even before *Elder Tales* went real, Akatsuki had not been "that guy who plays a character called Akatsuki in the game," but "a guy named Akatsuki who lives in this world," and everything he said or did in the game had reinforced that image. Calling it acting would have been rude. Role playing was part of the fun of games like *Elder Tales*, and there was no reason for other players to criticize it.

Besides, Shiroe thought Akatsuki was a pretty skilled player. He was quiet, curt, and didn't have a shred of personal charm—in that sense, he was very nearly the opposite of Marielle—but when Shiroe had been in parties with him, Akatsuki had performed his role flawlessly, and he'd never forgotten to be considerate to the other party members. Cheerful words and actions weren't the only ways to be considerate. Players like him were invaluable these days.

More than anything, Shiroe liked the fact that silences never got uncomfortable. In some relationships, silences tended to feel stony and strained, but Akatsuki and Shiroe were a bit alike in a few ways, and even when they'd hunted together for long stretches, the silence had never gotten awkward. Shiroe felt as if it was because they'd been communicating through something other than words, instead of simply being mute. They'd pieced together a conversation from small, intentional actions and exchanges: The timing of a team play, a slight gesture when providing support in combat, the rests between battles. An Assassin with a professional's pride who could be relied on during quests: That was Shiroe's image of Akatsuki.

"Hi, Akatsuki. Did you need something?"

Akatsuki got his intent across with a slight dip of his jaw, then withdrew into the depths of the shop, which looked set to come down around his ears. Apparently, this particular shop wasn't an independent zone; it was just a huge object within the Akiba boundaries.

Accepting Akatsuki's invitation, Shiroe and Naotsugu followed him into the dim ruin.

"Hey, Shiro. What sort of guy is this dude?" Naotsugu whispered.

"Akatsuki is a role player," Shiroe answered, also whispering. "He doesn't say much, but he's got skills. Solid ones... Under the circumstances, though, he's probably as depressed as the rest of us."

They'd already lost sight of Akatsuki; he'd gone deeper into the ruin by himself. His behavior seemed a bit more impatient than usual.

The room smelled damp and dusty. The morning sun streamed in through chinks in the crumbling walls and narrow windows in ruler-straight lines. The place really had been some sort of shop, most likely a restaurant: The room they'd entered was spacious and terribly jumbled, with several scattered tables, chairs, and sofas tipped over or resting at crazy angles.

Akatsuki turned then, staring at Naotsugu with eyes that seemed troubled and somehow accusatory.

Shiroe took that as his cue to make introductions.

"Akatsuki, this is Naotsugu. Guardian. He's an old friend of mine, and he's pretty reliable. You can trust him."

"Naotsugu here. Nice to meetcha! I dunno if you're an open type or a moody type, but whenever you want to talk about raunchy stuff, count me in."

It was a typical Naotsugu greeting: much too straightforward. *You just met this guy*, Shiroe thought, feeling very close to his wits' end, but

Akatsuki's expression was tense, as though he didn't have the emotional leeway to care.

Was Akatsuki always this on edge? Shiroe wondered privately, as the uneasy silence lengthened. *He didn't say much, but unless I'm remembering wrong, he used to be light on his feet and love fighting.*

"I've been looking for you."

At last, Akatsuki spoke, letting the words fall in a voice so faint it was barely audible. It was a very thin, unreliable voice.

"Did you need me for something?"

Akatsuki nodded silently in response to Shiroe's question. Even then, he seemed to be agonizing over something. He took two or three deep breaths, then spoke, as if he'd made up his mind.

"I want to buy your Appearance Reset Potion."

Akatsuki's voice was faint, but Shiroe heard what he said quite clearly. Even so, it took a while for the content of the words to travel from his ears to his brain, and he had to think for a bit before he really understood what he'd heard.

The Appearance Reset Potion was a limited-edition item that had been distributed at an event Shiroe had attended just after he'd started playing *Elder Tales*. It had been a free gift in some sort of sales promotion campaign intended to draw in more *Elder Tales* users. From what he remembered, the campaign itself had been a tie-up with online radio and a pretty shoddy affair. It was a badly designed event, with an appearance by some unknown, here-and-gone voice actor and the announcement of a new song thrown in haphazardly, and even the *Elder Tales* administration team probably wanted to forget it had ever happened.

Any game with a history of twenty years was bound to have several ridiculous campaigns in its past, and no doubt there were countless limited-edition items associated with those campaigns.

Elder Tales players created their characters right after they began the game. Eight races. Twelve classes. Name. Gender. Then there were other items to fine tune: height and body build, facial texture, hairstyle, hair and eye color. The "body build" category allowed players to adjust a dozen or so measurements, including chest diameter, leg length, and shoulder width. Of course, things like figures and faces had no effect whatsoever on battles, growth, or any other aspect of the game balance, so seasoned users tended to just punch in likely looking numbers and go.

The Appearance Reset Potion was exactly what it sounded like: an elixir that let players change the appearance of the characters they'd created at the beginning of the game. That said, since appearance didn't affect game difficulty at all, the potion was little better than a gag item. In line with the extremely shoddy sales promotion campaign, although it was incredibly rare, it was just a "fun" item with no practical significance.

…Until now.

"A-A-Akatsuki… D-don't tell me…"

Shiroe's tone earned him a very focused glare from Akatsuki.

"You're a girl?"

In sharp contrast with his intrepid, exquisitely skillful professional killer's looks, Akatsuki nodded his head meekly.

That faint voice. Akatsuki had been working hard to disguise it, but it had been a woman's voice. In this world, with text chats no longer an option, there was no way to hide it.

"…Okay. I did not see that coming."

Beside Shiroe, Naotsugu had frozen up, too.

▶ **3**

Shiroe made a trip to the bank and withdrew the Appearance Reset Potion from his deposit box. Back at the crumbling shop, he handed the item to Akatsuki. The Assassin looked visibly relieved to be holding the pale orange vial.

"Wait here."

Akatsuki disappeared into the shop's interior. *Interior* wasn't quite the right word for it; there were no other rooms farther back. There was a single-panel, freestanding screen at the border between the kitchen and the rest of the shop, and apparently Akatsuki's belongings were stashed behind it.

That's not safe, Shiroe thought. *Don't tell me he—uh, she—has actually been living here...* But the atmosphere was tense, and he knew better than to actually ask.

"Hey, Akatsuki. You okay back there?"

"Fine... Gkh!"

"What's wrong?"

"This potion...hurts. A lot."

Akatsuki seemed to have drunk the potion right away. An orange light the same color as the potion glowed from the shadows behind the screen. Akatsuki's response to Naotsugu had been tinged with pain, and that had worried Shiroe, but it was nothing compared to what came next. He felt his face go pale.

Sounds were leaking from behind the screen. Sounds like a whole bundle of chopsticks being snapped in two. Sounds like wet rags being ripped to shreds. Sounds so awful he didn't want to know how they were being made.

Whoa, hold it, no, that can't be okay—

"Ugkh...agh..."

Worried, Shiroe had started toward the screen, but Akatsuki's groan seemed to nail his feet to the floor. It certainly did sound like a woman's voice, and a very young woman at that. The strangled cries of pain continued, but Shiroe was paralyzed by the idea that if he kicked the screen out of the way he might accidentally see her naked.

Belatedly, Shiroe realized why Akatsuki had never used voice chat. Voice chat would have instantly telegraphed her gender to other players, and since she was role-playing as an Assassin, she would have found it terribly inconvenient.

"It takes all kinds, I guess."

Naotsugu sighed. He'd picked up a fallen stool, dusted it off, and sat down on it. Shiroe was startled, too, but it wasn't an inconceivable situation. In current online games, where voice chat was the main mode of communication, it wasn't common for players to play as characters of a different gender, but it wasn't as if it *never* happened. *Elder Tales* had a reputation for being complex and expertly executed, a game for experienced gamers. Both men and women enjoyed online games, but at least according to a statistic Shiroe had come across in a magazine article, women tended to prefer lighter games. In Shiroe's own experience, about 70 percent of the players in *Elder Tales* were male and only

30 percent were female. Akatsuki was a player who loved combat and had a detailed understanding of the system, so Shiroe had never suspected that "he" might actually be a "she."

"It's over. I'm okay—thank you."

The Akatsuki who emerged from behind the screen was a girl not quite 150 centimeters tall. She had long black hair that swayed as she moved, and as Shiroe had guessed from her voice, she was surprisingly lovely. Since she was more than thirty centimeters shorter than her former character, she seemed to be drowning in the black men's outfit that had fit her earlier character. She looked like a little kid who'd dressed up in her dad's work clothes. Still, there was something adorable about the delicate white ankles that peeked out of the thick, upturned cuffs and the tiny fingers poking out of the rolled-up sleeves.

"Whoa. It's an actual pretty girl. A real one."

Naotsugu's mouth hung halfway open as he muttered.

Shiroe had to agree.

In this world, basic figures and hairstyles seemed to have been inherited from the *Elder Tales* model settings. However, recent observations seemed to indicate that elements of their real-world counterparts had been blended in as well.

Shiroe's character in this world was a half Alv, a hybrid of the human and ancient Alv races. Alvs were supposed to be slender and brimming with curiosity, but when he'd checked the mirror at the inn, his face bore a marked resemblance to the one he wore back home in the real world. Since that resemblance included what people told him were his mean-looking *sanpaku* eyes, the discovery had left Shiroe rather depressed.

Unlike Shiroe, Akatsuki was a pure-blooded human, and if the same logic were applied to her, she was beautiful, full stop. Large black eyes in a pale oval face. Eyebrows like elegant arcs of deep black ink. If she looked like this even through the warped lens of the game world, the real Akatsuki must be incredibly lovely—the sort of girl anyone would call a beauty.

That said, Akatsuki's new body was quite small. The top of her head didn't reach Shiroe's shoulder, and she might not even have been 150 centimeters tall.

In *Elder Tales*, players had very fine control over the details of their Adventurer's figure and appearance. The male Akatsuki had been very tall.

He'd probably had at least thirty centimeters on the current Akatsuki. Shiroe's character was only a few centimeters taller than the real-world Shiroe, and even he'd had a hard time walking at first. The handicap the disaster had inflicted on Akatsuki must have been dozens of times worse.

Shiroe felt paralyzed. He hadn't expected her to be so pretty.

"...Nope. No way."

Naotsugu spoke, breaking the tension.

"I take back what I said. You can't be an open perv, a moody perv, or any kind of perv, because you're not a guy. You're one of them that *wears* the panties. Don't you forget it."

While that was no doubt true, it was an unreasonable declaration, and it seemed to puzzle Akatsuki.

"Lord Shiroe. Is this person deranged?"

"No, he isn't deranged, he's just... Um. He's just fundamentally weird."

"What about me is weird?!"

"Strange either way, then," Akatsuki said, watching Naotsugu out of the corner of her eye.

Possibly because the voice chat restriction had been lifted, Akatsuki's responses were much more relaxed than they had been when *Elder Tales* was a game. Still, the way she spoke—as if she was economizing on words—fit perfectly with Shiroe's mental image of Akatsuki.

...Although that cute voice of hers is really disorienting.

"Hey, I asked you a question! What about me is weird?! I was born one hundred percent male! What sort of guy would I be if I couldn't talk dirty once in a while? It's like my calling. Not that I'd expect a *girl* like you to understand..."

Naotsugu, puffing out his chest proudly over absolutely nothing, shot Akatsuki a look and snorted contemptuously.

"Still, that sounded pretty rough back there. Here. Drink up."

He tossed her a canteen filled with well water. Shiroe and Naotsugu had taken to buying well water because it was the cheapest thing there was, and everything else tasted just like it anyway.

"Thanks."

Akatsuki looked a bit surprised by the gesture. She probably couldn't figure out whether Naotsugu was a weirdo or a considerate type who was good at looking out for people. Still, she caught the canteen and gulped down quite a lot of its contents without coming up for air. Apparently she'd been really thirsty.

There in the damp-smelling shop, the three of them took up whatever positions felt comfortable and settled down to talk.

According to Akatsuki, she'd been living in this ruin for five days, trying to stay out of sight and unable to get much of anything to eat or drink. At first, Shiroe couldn't fathom why she'd do a thing like that, but as he listened to her story, he began to understand.

The difference between this body and Akatsuki's former one had been so large that she couldn't even walk well. She'd been able to sidle slowly around town, but if she'd gotten caught up in any trouble, she wouldn't have been able to cope with it, and she'd assumed that the probability of running into trouble was very high. In this world, with text chat no longer an option, if she wanted to buy anything or contact friends, she'd have to speak. She could have communicated by writing notes, but even that would have made people treat her with suspicion.

Of course, it wasn't as if the act of speaking carried a penalty. She would simply have been a man with a woman's voice. However, a tall, fierce killer who spoke with a woman's voice would have been a glaring contradiction, and the combination would undoubtedly have attracted attention. Akatsuki had expected trouble, and she probably would have gotten it.

"Then I remembered that earlier when I was in a party with Lord Shiroe, he'd mentioned an Appearance Reset Potion. I thought, if I had that, I could at least get myself out of this mess."

"I see," Naotsugu said.

"…Still. I think you should've just played as this midget model version to begin with."

"Don't call me a midget."

Akatsuki gave Naotsugu a sharp glare. She had a very forceful gaze. It had been forceful before she drank the potion, too, but now that she had her own form back, her incredibly serious gaze, loaded with willpower, was so persuasive that Shiroe thought it could probably bore a hole through solid rock.

It didn't seem to bother Naotsugu, though.

"Ain't nothing wrong with calling a midget 'midget,' short stuff."

"I don't want to hear that from a weirdo."

It was very like Naotsugu to casually pull food and drink from his pack and offer them to her, giving her what she seemed to need even as he teased her, Shiroe thought. Akatsuki seemed to realize that, too. She didn't seriously snap at him, and she seemed a bit out of her element.

"Part of what makes games fun is being able to do things you can't do in real life, you know?" she said, sulking a bit. "Just like with fantasy and sci-fi. For me, that 'thing' was being tall."

When she put it that way, she had a very good point.

"Well, yeah. I guess there's no help for that."

Naotsugu's voice was superficially sympathetic. He shot a glance at Akatsuki.

"……"

"Yep, there's no help for that. It's not your fault, Akatsuki. I'm on your side here. Everybody's got the right to dream."

At that, he smiled as if he understood everything, then flashed her a thumbs-up. In the next instant, Akatsuki had hit him square in the face with an elegant flying knee kick.

"*No knees!* Did you seriously have to use your knee?!"

"Lord Shiroe, may I knee kick the weirdo?"

"You already did it! Don't ask for permission *now*!"

On seeing that exchange, Shiroe was unable to choke back a laugh. That they didn't look as though they were actually on bad terms made it even funnier.

"Way to score points by being a good lil boy all by yourself," Naotsugu accused.

"Would you keep this weirdo on a tighter leash?" Akatsuki demanded.

After choking back his laughter more successfully for a little while, Shiroe turned to Akatsuki.

"It is easier being in a body that's more like your own, isn't it?"

Akatsuki considered the question for a minute, then answered with the too-serious expression Shiroe was beginning to expect.

"The male body looked really neat, and its reach was much better, but…there were issues."

"Yeah? What was the problem?" Naotsugu asked.

These two hadn't met before, but they already seemed to have gotten used to each other. From what Shiroe could remember, Akatsuki tended to be cautious about human relationships, but Naotsugu's Naotsugu-ness seemed to have disarmed her somewhat.

"Um… Using the bathroom."

Akatsuki looked down, mumbling.

Naotsugu! That's sexual harassment!!

"Oh, right. Because you had a wiener!"

Naotsugu! Don't make it worse!

"Um. So, uh. Changing the subject! The measurements of this version are closer to your real body, right?"

Shiroe asked, executing a supremely clumsy change of topic in an attempt to help out Akatsuki, who'd gone red and was looking very uncomfortable. Even for a woman, she was quite short.

"Yes."

Akatsuki nodded, tugging at bits of her baggy clothes, her expression earnest.

Part of that's probably to hide her embarrassment over Naotsugu's dirty old man comments, but…

Even then, Shiroe thought, she was an oddly serious girl. She had a habit of keeping her eyes fixed too long on whatever she was looking at. When she looked at people or things, she looked so hard she seemed to be staring. The habit had probably belonged to the real Akatsuki in their former world, and it gave the slight girl an earnest, desperate air.

"That means the height difference problem is solved, then. It's easier to walk now, isn't it?"

"Yes. Thank you," Akatsuki said in concise gratitude.

Her brusque tone, her abruptness, her habit of gazing fixedly at things. In Shiroe's mind, that combination was gradually overlapping with his image of the old Akatsuki, the taciturn, professional fighter. Physically, they couldn't have been more different, but her serious behavior seemed to him to be the very essence of Akatsuki. Little by little, he felt the gap between the slender girl in front of him and the Akatsuki he knew close.

"How much should I pay you? Will everything I have be enough?"

Akatsuki asked Shiroe a hair-raising question, fixing him with a gaze that was just this side of a glare.

"I only have about thirty thousand… Could you settle for that?"

"You don't need to…"

"I can't possibly not pay you. You said that potion was a limited-edition event item. That means it's rare. You can't get it anymore. That item was technically priceless. I know thirty thousand doesn't even begin to pay for it."

Her logic was correct. Up until now, the item had just been sitting around in his safe-deposit box, but under the circumstances, he could easily have asked a king's ransom for it.

"……"

"……"

Still, even if that was true, was it important enough to clean out someone's account over? Shiroe had serious doubts about that. The item had been completely useless until a few days ago.

"Um. Well… Would you settle for free?"

"I don't wish to be labeled an ingrate."

Akatsuki's searing upturned gaze, the gesture that gave the impression that she was staring at him, made Shiroe pretty uncomfortable. That it belonged to a very pretty girl made it practically lethal.

"If you're that worried about it, just give him some panties as a thank— Ghk—"

Akatsuki's small knee made another graceful touchdown on Naotsugu's face. Granted, Naotsugu was sitting on a pile of rubble, but even so, the kick struck home at a good angle.

"You're quite an athlete, Miss Akatsuki."

"Wha— Hey! Moody perv! Whose side are you on?"

"Lord Shiroe. May I knee this pervert?"

"Look, I told you, ask *before* you kick!"

Akatsuki pointed at Naotsugu, asking for permission. The gesture struck Shiroe as cute, and he smiled in spite of himself.

"Whatever. Never mind. Forget about how much the potion costs. Hey, Akatsuki."

"We are not on first-name terms."

"That's not important, either, short stuff."

"Don't call me 'short stuff,' and *yes,* this is *very* important," Akatsuki insisted stubbornly. "If I've swindled Lord Shiroe into giving me his limited-edition item for free, I will have brought everlasting shame upon myself."

Naotsugu looked at the sulking Akatsuki, then glanced at Shiroe, then looked from him to Akatsuki again. Then he continued.

"No, that's a pointless subject if ever there was one. Forget that, Akatsuki. Listen, why don't you travel around with us for a while?"

"—Huh?"

The words seemed to have been the last thing Akatsuki had expected. She froze so abruptly it was as if she'd been put on pause.

"Counselor. Explain."

Having said his piece, Naotsugu tossed the ball to Shiroe, as if the rest of it was his job.

Thanks a lot. We didn't discuss this, and I have no idea what you want me to do, Shiroe thought, but he did approve of the proposal itself.

"…Hm. Yes, I don't think it's a bad idea."

However, thinking that it wasn't a bad idea didn't necessarily make it easy to explain. He was sure Naotsugu's intentions had been good, but intentions aside, an undeniable air of embarrassment hung about the proposal. It felt as if he'd lost a penalty game and was being forced to pick up girls.

"…I hate to say this, but you're a girl, Akatsuki, and you're small. Even with your old body back, you— Uh, I mean, your appearance and voice may be consistent now, but you might get caught up in unpleasantness anyway… Maybe. On top of that, you aren't part of a guild yet. Is there one you'd like to join?"

"I don't like belonging to things. Assassins are lone wolves by nature."

Akatsuki's face clouded; she seemed to be thinking hard.

"Yeah, I guess you would be. We're a lot like that ourselves. Free-lance adventurers. We do whatever we want. Free panties freedom."

"…Shut up, pervert."

"If you have somewhere in mind, that's one thing, but… From what I hear, unaffiliated players are being hassled these days. The big guilds are trying to build up their ranks, and they're scouting players right and left. I think female players probably get it even worse than male players."

"Really…?"

"A place to sleep, the chance to pool information on the situation… It wouldn't hurt to be a little connected, under the circumstances."

Akatsuki nodded.

Besides, it's not as if Akatsuki's terribly good with people…

Shiroe didn't consider himself to be very good with people, either, but Akatsuki's unsociability was off the charts. When *Elder Tales* was still a game, Akatsuki's way of being considerate had been to word-lessly help people out when they needed it. Shiroe knew her brusque-ness didn't mean she was unfriendly, but the vast majority of players probably wouldn't pick up on that. Akatsuki was a fighter, and as far as Shiroe knew, she had very few acquaintances. He suspected he might be the one who'd worked with her the most.

Of course, that was just another way to play, and when this had been a game, it hadn't been a problem. In a game, the only "right" way for a person to play was the way that let them have the most fun, provided they didn't cause trouble for other people.

However, the current world wasn't a game, and Akatsuki's brusque-ness was bound to cause trouble, especially since she'd turned out to be so pretty.

I don't know whether Naotsugu thought things through that far, but… it's another good reason for her to stick with us for a while—except…

"Hey, why not? Assassins are good at offing people sneakily, right? While we're fighting, you can creep up behind the monster and shank it. It'll be the perfect combo play. Death-to-evildoers city," Naotsugu said happily.

Well, he's right about the teamwork, at least… What kind of crazy "city" would that be?

"Hm. Would you be all right with that, Lord Shiroe?"

"Absolutely. Things will feel safer if there are three of us anyway."

For a moment, Akatsuki hesitated. Then she turned that peculiar, straightforward, laser-like gaze on him and nodded.

"I see. Then I'll serve you as your ninja, Lord Shiroe… My liege."

Ninja?

…Liege?

Wasn't Akatsuki an Assassin?

Although those questions did cross his mind, the proposal seemed like a good one to Shiroe.

"I owe you for saving me from my forced sex-reassignment crisis, and it is my duty to repay you with equivalent labor. This is how I'll do it. From now on, my liege, I'll protect you as your ninja."

Akatsuki murmured. Uncharacteristically, her gaze wandered restlessly, as if she was ill at ease.

Naotsugu had a purple bruise spreading around his nose, but it didn't seem to faze him; he was watching Shiroe and smirking.

"All righty, then. We're a team. Welcome aboard, short stuff."

"Shut up, idiot."

"We're a very mismatched trio, but never mind. I look forward to working with you."

In the dingy store, its interior shot through with shafts of golden light, Shiroe and the others clinked their canteens together, toasting the formation of their team.

▶ **4**

Several days had passed since Akatsuki had joined them. Shiroe, Naotsugu, and Akatsuki were gradually shifting their activities into the field zones near Akiba. There were several reasons for the move, one of which was that when Shiroe and Naotsugu had gotten up the courage to go to the Forest of Library Towers, the battles had been much harder than they'd anticipated.

Battles in this world were faithful replicas of their *Elder Tales* counterparts where fundamental structure and strategy were concerned, but they were very different when it came to individual participants' tactics and combat techniques. The battles included a vast number of subtle elements that players had no control over in the game, such as sword swings, the angle at which shields were thrust out, footholds, and movement. Issues with fields of vision and difficulty in fighting together were also big problems. Worst of all were the mental hurdles, especially the terror.

The first time he and Naotsugu went out to a field zone, Shiroe's impression had been that this was going to be pretty rough. After several one-day expeditions, he'd revised that impression to *Conventional strategies won't be enough.*

However, Akatsuki was completely specialized to vanguard work, and in terms of surviving in this world, the sooner they got used to fighting, the better. They'd decided to stay together for the moment, but there was no telling whether or not it would last. The three of them had decided it would be best to get the basics of combat nailed down now while they were together.

The Crescent Moon League guild was another reason. Since that first visit, Shiroe and the others had made frequent trips to the guild-hall to trade information. Unlike their trio, the Crescent Moon League had artisan players as well. Shiroe's own subclass was Scribe, and he'd worked his way up to a high level, but the guild had a variety of other artisans and more members in general. These players had connections around Akiba, and they were able to gather information in town more efficiently than Shiroe could in the same amount of time. In terms of exchanging information, it was better for Shiroe's group to investigate various things in the field zones and work at practical training while they were there.

Of course, self-preservation instincts had compelled several people to begin doing what Shiroe and the others were doing, but Akiba still overflowed with apathetic players. Even now, a full week later, they seemed unable to believe the situation. They probably thought that someone—a god or the administrators—would rescue them.

Or maybe they "think" that because they wouldn't be able to stand it otherwise, not because they really believe it.

It wasn't a feeling Shiroe couldn't relate to. He just wasn't optimistic enough to be able to believe in that hope.

If this was some sort of prank and help found them someday, fine. If that happened, Shiroe would be relieved, too. His university hadn't been all that comfortable, but it was the world where he'd been born and raised, and he was used to it. Of course, he wanted to go back.

However, even if this situation had been orchestrated by the administrators, there was an undeniable possibility that the incident had been irreversible and that things would never go back to normal. Shiroe was cautious to the point of pessimism, and he couldn't bet everything on the possibility of rescue and spend his days sitting around.

Akiba was the largest city on the Japanese server and the starting point for new players. As with every player city, the zones in its immediate area were comparatively easy even for beginners to work their way through, and there were many safe places where only low-level monsters appeared. Shiroe and his group planned to check each of these beginner zones and gradually work their way up to high-level zones. In terms of simple level, Shiroe, Naotsugu, and Akatsuki were all level 90. In low-level beginner zones, even if they were attacked by monsters, they'd take hardly any damage. In addition, if the enemy sensed the sort of power they had, they wouldn't attack recklessly. That technically would have made it possible to avoid battles with monsters entirely, but Shiroe and the others went out of their way to fight as many different monsters as they could.

Although the enemy's attacks weren't much of a threat in and of themselves, when various monsters leapt at them, they'd always cringe back at first. When they'd gamed through a monitor, they hadn't known anything about the beasts' harsh breathing or the choking stench of blood or what it was like to be targeted by something that wanted to kill them. Even if the enemy was a low-level monster, the terrors of real battle were enough to make them recoil. A monster might be so insignificant that they wouldn't earn any experience points by defeating it, but even so, if it wasn't one they'd fought before, Shiroe's group battled it several times to study its habits and learn how best to handle it.

Naotsugu was always in the lead in their basic battle formation. Battles began with Naotsugu charging the enemy and closing the distance. As a Guardian, Naotsugu used his shield skills and the heavy armor he was so proud of to block enemy attacks. Taunting Shout was a basic Guardian skill that had the effect of sending monsters into a frenzy. The enraged monsters would attack Naotsugu ferociously, which kept them from targeting Shiroe or Akatsuki.

However, as they'd expected, keeping an eye on statuses while swinging a sword and paying out fierce attacks on the front line was no easy task. Back when *Elder Tales* had been a game, all you had to do was specify which monster you wanted to attack, and your character would attack it automatically and repeatedly. Enemy attacks were also dodged using evasion skills; characters would dodge with a set probability of success, deflect attacks with their swords, or stop them with their shields, and in all cases, the player didn't need to do anything. If you wanted to use a special technique, all you had to do was click on an icon.

When actually fighting in this other world, though, they needed to either step in or jump back when a real-life monster appeared in front of them, and they had to bring both hands down over and over again to beat it with weapons. When they fought a monster that had come right up to them, their field of vision narrowed, and it was often hard to see what the monster was doing. After much discussion, Shiroe, Naotsugu, and Akatsuki came up with several formations and strategy codes. They came to the conclusion that it was safest for Shiroe to give orders to the other two, since he was away from the front line and had a clear view of the whole area.

As Shiroe used his spells to provide support, he watched the surrounding area and kept an eye on his friends' statuses. Many of the Enchanter spells were fairly humdrum. One of the rare spells that Enchanters could really boast about to the other classes was Keen Edge: Its effect raised the attack force of companions' weapons by 30 percent or so, and since the effect lasted several hours, there was no need to recast during battle.

There were many other spells he could use, of course, but he used the rest only as the situation demanded while he kept an eye on the battle. For now, Shiroe's main role was to keep a wary eye on the area and to watch his friends' statuses.

After several battles, Akatsuki seemed to have gotten used to working with Shiroe and Naotsugu. Assassin was one of the three Weapon Attack classes, and its ability to inflict maximum damage instantaneously was the highest of all twelve classes. Unlike the Warriors, which were skilled at drawing enemy attacks on the front lines, the Weapon Attack classes had comparatively low Defense, and they weren't good at drawing the enemy to them. That meant that their role was to defeat the enemies the Warriors attracted. Of the Weapon Attack classes, Assassins had abilities engineered to quickly eliminate enemies. In a word, they were killing machines. The Assassin certain-kill technique Assassinate could inflict close to ten thousand in damage instantaneously.

Akatsuki seemed to skim over battlefields. Her slight body was astonishingly nimble, and even when she was sprinting to close in on an enemy, her shape seemed to blur to the point where it was sometimes hard to see her at all. According to Akatsuki, this was an Assassin technique known as Stealth Walk, and it raised the success rate of attacks launched right after capturing the enemy's blind spot. As she ran, her black hair streaming, she moved with an almost liquid smoothness, and she was so graceful that sometimes they couldn't help but stare. When Naotsugu blocked the enemy's fangs with his shield, then used it to knock them back, she had them skewered with her short sword in moments. When an enemy was considering an attack on some opening in Naotsugu's guard, she'd slash them in the side and ward off the attack.

While vanguard and rearguard team plays were big picture and strategic, vanguard-vanguard team plays were terribly direct and aggressive. For that very reason, they needed enough actual experience to understand one another's habits by instinct.

Meanwhile, Shiroe watched their statuses, issued orders for battle maneuvers to curb enemy movements, and sometimes used his range of Enchanter's spells to bind the enemy or to trick them and give his friends the advantage.

By the end of a week, Shiroe, Naotsugu, and Akatsuki were battling level-50 monsters.

CHAPTER.
3
BATTLE OF ROKA

▶ LEVEL: **90**

▶ RACE: **HUMAN**

▶ CLASS: **ASSASSIN**

▶ HP: **9873**

▶ MP: **9771**

▶ ITEM 1:

[KIIN-TURNED TENMOKU SWORD]

A BLACK CERAMIC BLADE
WITH A BEAUTIFUL
PATTERN RUNNING DOWN
ITS LENGTH. THE BLACK
GLAZE KEEPS IT FROM
REFLECTING LIGHT, MAKING
IT EASIER TO CONCEAL.
THIS ITEM IS PRODUCED BY
AFICIONADOS.

▶ ITEM 2:

[BLACK COSTUME OF ETERNAL NIGHT]

NINJA CLOTHES IN COLORS THAT MELT INTO THE
DARKNESS. EQUIPPED WITH A SPECIAL MAGICAL
POWER THAT RAISES THE ABILITIES
OF THE PERSON WEARING
THEM IN PROPORTION TO
THE DARKNESS OF THE
SURROUNDING AREA. IT'S
STANDARD TO USE THEM
WITH DARKNESS SPELLS OR
NIGHT-VISION EQUIPMENT.

▶ ITEM 3:

[HELIOTROPE HAIRPIN]

AN ORNAMENT THAT RAISES
YOUR LUCK VALUES AND
MAGICAL DEFENSE. HAS
AN EFFECT, VOLUNTARILY
ACTIVATED, THAT
DESTROYS THE PIN BUT
FANS THE ANIMOSITY OF THE
MONSTERS IN THE AREA. IN
THE LANGUAGE OF FLOWERS, *HELIOTROPE*
MEANS "FAITHFUL HEART, DEVOTED LOVE."

-190
-180
-170
160
-150

<Potion>
An elixir. You won't feel truly
safe without it, but if you take
it along, you won't use it.

► 1

"Now *that's* what I call a hunt. What a haul."

Naotsugu swung the hatchet he'd been using to harvest items, wiped off the blood, and returned it to its sheath.

As Shiroe nodded in agreement, he lowered his staff, canceling the waiting spells.

...I'd better watch it. I managed to depress myself remembering all that.

He shrugged, sighing. He felt troubled. That said, there'd been so many troubling things since they came to this world that even he wasn't quite clear on what was troubling him now.

Man, I hope that doesn't turn into something I say all the time.

"What's wrong, my liege?"

Akatsuki had come up beside Shiroe while his mind was elsewhere; she seemed to have finished getting her pack in order. She gazed up into his face with eyes as lustrous as polished obsidian. It was unnerving. Shiroe gave an evasive smile, then suggested that they start heading back.

At only a kilometer per side, Smallstone Herb Garden, the field zone they were in, wasn't very big. It was already dusk. The wind that blew across the forest and ruined buildings was chilly, and the only sound in the area was faint, scattered birdsong. This particular zone was close to both Akiba and the town of Shibuya, which made it convenient for day-trip hunting excursions. Although it was close to a player town, it held relatively high-level monsters.

"Okay, then, let's head home."

"Understood."

Black-clad Akatsuki answered Shiroe in her usual unemotional, too-serious tone and picked up the pack she'd set down, slinging it back over her shoulder.

The area was littered with the carcasses of the Triffids and Brier Weasels they'd been fighting. After a short while, the corpses dissolved into sparks of light and vanished.

Triffids were walking plants with buds that looked exactly like rugby balls at their tips. These monsters were horror movie material: If a human came near, the rugby ball split open into three sections, revealing a maw bristling with rows of sharp fangs like shards of broken glass. Brier Weasels were mottled purple-and-green monsters that lived parasitically on briers. They were fast, launching briers at players and moving with even more agility than cats.

The monsters' levels were 48 and 52. These were fairly high levels for *Elder Tales* monsters, but they were still forty levels below Shiroe's group. They wouldn't get any experience points from defeating them.

During their training over the past few days, Shiroe, Naotsugu, and Akatsuki had learned that the *Elder Tales* specs were reproduced fairly faithfully in this world. They still weren't sure, but they suspected that a monster would have to be five levels below them—in other words, level 85—for them to earn any experience points by defeating it. However, if the three of them together were able to defeat a level 85 monster at all at this point, it would be a very close fight. Besides, although one level-85 monster would be tough enough, monsters tended to attack in groups.

"You okay?"

"Yeah, I'm fine. I chugged a potion. The Great Naotsugu's Defense is an iron fortress, like that one mecha. Steel city."

Naotsugu grinned and struck the armor he was wearing. Since his fist was sheathed in a dull gray gauntlet as well, it made a heavy, hollow sound.

According to Naotsugu, the pain from enemy attacks was far less than what it would be in the real world. He said that even when his HP fell below 50 percent, instead of feeling half-dead, he felt as though he was covered in hot, swollen, stinging bruises. As Naotsugu put it, the very worst pain was about as bad as whacking your little toe on the corner of your dresser.

I think I'd be in tears by the third time that happened, though.

Shiroe had frowned slightly at Naotsugu's words, but Naotsugu himself had laughed, loud and long.

Still, just because it's that way now doesn't necessarily mean it will stay that way, Shiroe thought as he stood guard. *We're still fighting low-level enemies at this point, and we don't take a lot of damage all at once. We have the time to make careful decisions during battle, and we can fight without paying too much attention to securing a path of retreat. If we keep fighting higher-level enemies, though, we'll probably start taking more damage... If that happens, no matter how good Naotsugu is at what he does, he may not have as much leeway as he does now. I'd better come up with some other possibilities now, while there's time...*

The Guardian class was noted for being the cornerstone of the front line and for having the highest HP and Defense of all twelve classes. If there was any damage that Naotsugu couldn't withstand, it was a sure bet that none of the other classes would be able to.

Which means... It really would be good to have a healer around. Still, I'd rather not pull someone else in just for efficiency's sake. If we asked someone to join up with a motive like that, we might not be able to work together well. And anyway, even if something wipes us out, we'll just get sent back to the town. But...

This world held the miracle of resurrection from death. Shiroe and the others knew that if they died they'd be resurrected in Akiba's great temple. Even so, it didn't make them feel like being reckless. Even if it came with a guarantee of recovery in this world, death was still abhorrent and impossible to accept.

The idea of coming back to life after dying is seriously creepy.

"My liege...?"

"Hey, Shiro. Let's hurry up and get home."

Several days had passed since the three of them had started traveling together, and the group dynamics were turning out to be far better than Shiroe had expected. Maybe each of them had only convinced themselves that they worked best on their own. Maybe they'd actually been suited to living like this.

That said, that very aptitude made their various personalities stand out in sharper relief. In this particular group, Shiroe naturally became the one who worried.

Of course, since I've been in charge of strategy ever since the Debauchery Tea Party, I guess that hasn't changed...

Shiroe tended to involuntarily retreat into his own thoughts. Even he was aware that it might not be a good habit, but he didn't feel as if it was something he really had to change.

I don't mind being the guy who worries, he thought. *I just don't want to be the gloom-and-doom guy.*

"All right. Let's move out... Does anybody need more light?"

Shiroe was preparing his Magic Light spell as he spoke.

"No, my liege Shiro."

"I don't supposed you'd stop the 'my liege' business, would you? Just call me Shiroe. We're friends, you know."

"In that case, you call me Akatsuki, too. No Miss."

Letting his request go nearly unacknowledged, Akatsuki stared at Shiroe.

That gaze of hers is just too much... Agh.

Personally, Shiroe thought Akatsuki was cute. Most people would probably call Akatsuki a lovely girl, even if they didn't know her at all. Still, he couldn't take that way she had of watching him fixedly with those dead-serious eyes. It wasn't that he didn't like her, not at all. It was just that she made him very uncomfortable.

Shiroe was a genuine indoors-type online gamer. He wasn't one for socializing, and of course, he didn't have an abundance of experience with the opposite sex.

I guess that's just an excuse, though. When it comes down to it... Well, stuff like that makes me embarrassed and I'm bad at it, that's all... I mean, how could I not be? Yeah. I know. Even I know, but still.

"My liege."

As if to compound Shiroe's confusion, Akatsuki stepped in front of him and called to him. The height difference was huge, and there was something terribly embarrassing about having her look up at him.

"Umm, er, what? —Hey, Naotsugu, quit smirking!"

Taking a verbal jab at Naotsugu, who was watching him and laughing, Shiroe motioned for Akatsuki to go on.

"I'll act as a scout on the way home."

"Why?"

"Practice. One of the special Assassin techniques is Night Vision, and I also have Sneak and Silent Move. I want to see how it feels to use them here. The forest will be the perfect place."

As Akatsuki spoke, she glanced into the woods, where the dusk was already beginning to thicken, and refastened the black belt that held her sheathed short sword, getting ready.

Solo movement?

After giving it a little thought, Shiroe granted permission. This zone didn't appear to have any monsters stronger than the two types they'd fought earlier. Akatsuki could fight them one-on-one and not lose, and even if they attacked in a group, she'd probably be able to run away. Besides, he understood her impulse to test the skills she had. She wanted to be able to enter future situations fully prepared. Having a solid grasp of their abilities was a prerequisite for survival.

"Just don't get careless. Meet up with us again near the south gate. We'll be using Magic Light, so come find us instead of the other way around."

"Understood. If we're in the same zone, I'll know where you are."

Individuals who'd joined a party and were in the same zone as other members could use angle and distance information to tell where those members were. They probably wouldn't have any trouble meeting up again.

"See ya, short stuff."

"Shut up, stupid Naotsugu."

In the next instant, leaving that comeback behind her, Akatsuki melted into the trees.

"Not bad, short stuff."

Naotsugu looked as if he might whistle in appreciation.

"I didn't even hear leaves rustling."

Shiroe shrugged, chanting the Magic Light spell. A magical glow about as bright as a regular lamp flickered to life at the tip of his staff.

The sun wasn't quite down yet, but the magic lamp cast a soft light in the forest's dense undergrowth and deep orange dusk.

"We should head out, too."

"Roger that, Counselor. Forward march, let's book."

Shiroe and Naotsugu started through the forest in a bubble of warm light, heading for the eastern gate. Crunching frost-damp ribbons of green grass underfoot, they followed a deer track littered with mossy rocks through the forest of the Imperial Gardens.

It feels as if we're deep in the forests of Yakushima or the Amazon, like the ones I saw on WebTV. People say this could be another world, but I dunno... It's pretty hard to believe.

He could hear the faint, pleasant sound of insect chirps and clicks. The two of them parted the undergrowth as they advanced through the dark woods, Naotsugu sometimes using his longsword to cut through a particularly stubborn patch.

"So Akatsuki's a Tracker, huh?"

At Naotsugu's words, Shiroe remembered what Akatsuki had said. The special techniques she'd mentioned, Sneak and Silent Move, were Tracker abilities. Tracker was one of *Elder Tales*'s myriad subclasses, and it gave anyone who acquired it special abilities tailored to pursuit or tracking.

In *Elder Tales*, subclasses gave players convenient ability sets that weren't directly related to combat. They were completely independent of the main twelve combat-related classes, and as long as they fulfilled the conditions, any Adventurer could acquire a wide range of sub-classes, no matter what their main class was.

In general terms, subclasses could be divided into two basic types. One type included Chef, Tailor, Blacksmith, and Woodworker and other production-related subclasses. Players with these subclasses could create a wide variety of items by using facilities and the appropriate materials. Production-related subclasses were easy to acquire: All you had to do was purchase manuals from artisan non-player characters in the urban zones and then accumulate experience points in that line of work. This sort of experience was completely separate from combat experience, and although it took an extremely long time to advance to a high level, players didn't have to complete any particular quest or acquire any special item to do so. If they were patient, anyone could improve to the top of their subclass, and it didn't really require help from friends.

Shiroe's subclass was Scribe. Scribe was a production-related subclass that let players copy maps, documents, and books of spells. Its tools were paper and pen, and it was basically desk work.

The other type was role-play related: Subclass examples included Aristocrat, Merchant, and Rose Garden Princess. Unlike the production subclasses, role-play subclasses didn't allow players to create items, but they did grant several special abilities and unusual techniques, and they occasionally gave players special equipment. Akatsuki's Tracker was one such subclass. It granted the abilities to move silently, follow enemies or other players, and make one's presence impossible to detect.

Shiroe didn't know all that much about Trackers. The twelve main classes that were directly related to combat had been designed down to the details by the huge American corporation that had developed *Elder Tales*, and their abilities were adjusted frequently. In contrast, several subclasses were added with each expansion pack, and some had been independently added by subcontractors such as Fushimi Online Entertainment, the company that administered the Japanese server.

Although there were only twelve main classes, Shiroe could think of more than fifty subclasses, and that was just off the top of his head. Taking into account the fact that other subclasses existed on different servers, there was really no telling how many there actually were.

Of course, the powerful, convenient subclasses tended to get talked about and people swarmed to acquire them, so they were easy to remember. That meant it was possible to have a decent grasp of the abilities those subclasses granted, but even veteran players like Shiroe didn't know the abilities of all the minor subclasses.

In that jumble of good and bad, Tracker was a subclass that enjoyed modest recognition. It granted fairly convenient special abilities, but they weren't the sort that players would use regularly or even frequently. This exquisite balance placed it solidly in the middle, on the line between the major and minor subclasses. Players who weren't hard-core gamers like Shiroe might not know about it, but it was more famous than, say, Sailor or Janitor.

"She certainly knows how to specialize."

Naotsugu guffawed and told Shiroe he had *that* right.

I mean, she's an Assassin and a Tracker. She's way too into this. With a combination like that, I'm not surprised she called herself a ninja.

He and Naotsugu had a good laugh over Akatsuki's single-mindedness. The term "role-play" tended to be associated with ham acting, but when combined with her serious character, Akatsuki's version suited her far too well.

"How does she look to you, Shiro? …Little Miss Short Stuff, I mean."

"She's very agile on the front lines. She has great concentration."

It took a little while for Shiroe to find the words to answer the question Naotsugu hadn't quite asked.

He was asking for Shiroe's opinion of Akatsuki.

Shiroe's personal opinion of Akatsuki was as high as ever. He'd sounded brusque simply because it embarrassed him to praise her.

"Forget about me. What about you, Naotsugu? Are things harder, easier…?"

"—Easier. Our kill-off speed is in a whole different league from what it was when it was just you and me," Naotsugu said as he walked ahead of Shiroe. "Sometimes I'll turn around to take on another monster and it's dead already. She may be a midget, but she's a tough midget."

Naotsugu was a fundamentally frank, cheerful, sociable guy who could make friends with anybody in very little time. He did have a tendency to make off-color remarks, but Shiroe had a hunch that he did it at least partly on purpose to lighten the mood. Still, when it came to combat, he never gave praise he didn't mean. Naotsugu would choose words that wouldn't hurt the other person, but he wouldn't lie. Compared to all the evaluations Shiroe could remember him giving in the past, the one he'd just given Akatsuki was very nearly perfect.

"Akatsuki says that changing her form shortened her reach and that she isn't able to put much force behind her attacks. What do you think?"

"I wouldn't know about the reach. I've never gone midget myself. With speed and agility like that, though, reach can't be much of a handicap. Try taking one of those flying knee kicks. I swear she teleports. Even if you brace for it, she moves so fast you can't track it."

"I'll pass on that, thanks."

Naotsugu massaged his nose, as if the conversation had reminded him.

"If she says her attacks don't have as much force behind them, I'd guess she'd know. The game system says gender doesn't affect damage, but this is some other world, and maybe weight does add power to attacks... Or maybe it doesn't. Either way, it's a feeling, and only the person with the feeling knows what it feels like... Even then, though, you could make up for that lost power with a support spell, right? I mean, this is you we're talking about."

Naotsugu pushed some big, fernlike leaves up and out of the way as he spoke.

I guess he's right about that... Maybe.

Of the twelve main classes in *Elder Tales*, three were Warrior types, three were Weapon Attack types, three were Recovery types, and three were Magic Attack types. Shiroe's class, Enchanter, was one of the magic-user classes. Of the three, it was the one most specialized for support and tricky maneuvering, and it had all sorts of spells for reinforcing allies' abilities. Keen Edge increased weapon attack power. Sewn-Bind Hostage was an attack spell that throttled the enemy with cursed brambles every time an ally's weapon attack hit home. Mind Shock stunned the enemy's astral body, paralyzing them for a set amount of time. Enchanters were unconventional magic users who contributed to victories by supporting their allies and controlling the situation.

"...Well... There's that," Shiroe answered awkwardly.

Enchanter was the least popular class in *Elder Tales*. It couldn't have been valued less. Of course, Shiroe had chosen this class because he liked it, and he didn't feel the need to apologize for it to anybody. No matter what anyone said, he thought Enchanters were useful and that they held great potential. Still, even Shiroe understood that Enchanters couldn't perform at their best when they worked alone.

Needing friends meant that Enchanters' potential changed drastically depending on how well they got along with their companions. This wasn't a class performance issue. When working with other people to achieve a goal, game system values weren't a good measure of strength. Since Shiroe was fully aware of this, having someone tell him, "You're fine the way you are," and "It's okay for you to be here," made him feel terribly self-conscious. Being recognized for one's skills as an Enchanter was the same as having someone acknowledge a person's actual personality and relationships.

"...Listen. Shiro."

"Hm?"

"Nothin' specific, but...I don't think you really need to hold back as much as you do."

"Huh?"

Naotsugu had been walking in the lead, parting the underbrush, when he let those words fall. They were so far removed from what they'd been talking about earlier that Shiroe had no idea what he meant.

"...Like panties?"

"And you phrased that as a question because...?"

"Shiro, cute girls' enigmatic triangles are always posing questions to the universe. Learn to listen, you moody closet perfect-pervert-storm!"

"Just how girl crazy do you think I am anyway?!"

Shiroe didn't understand Naotsugu's friendly advice, at least not then. All he could do was follow his receding back.

At that point, Shiroe was still only an Enchanter.

▶ 2

After Shiroe and Naotsugu met back up with Akatsuki, they crossed into the next zone. Naotsugu was tired from the day's constant battling, but he was in a good mood. He turned and yelled back to the other two.

"Step it up, okay? The inn's calling my name."

The name of the zone was the Kanda Irrigation Canal. It was a ruin based on the Marunouchi train line in the real world and was currently inhabited by goblins, orcs, and other demihumans. That said, the levels of the goblins and orcs in this zone were in the low thirties, and they posed no threat to Shiroe's group. With this much of a level difference, the monsters wouldn't attack unless they had no other option.

The sun had set completely, and Naotsugu, Shiroe, and Akatsuki were beginning to regret having stayed so long in the Imperial Gardens forest. Since the monsters wouldn't attack recklessly, they could have found a suitable ruin or a likely looking grove and camped there for the night, but instead they walked down the highway, which was littered with abandoned cars and dump trucks, under the glow of the Magic Light. Akatsuki had insisted that, if they were going to sleep anyway, they'd sleep better in a place with real beds. Either way, their packs were stuffed with monster hides, fangs, and other loot. They had magic items they'd taken from the monsters as well, and they'd have to go back to town to cash them in.

Naotsugu was in the lead, and every so often, he'd turn around to check on Shiroe and Akatsuki.

It doesn't look like they're having any trouble walking. No matter what they say, they have stamina to spare. It must be the level-90 thing again.

That was a relief.

Unlike the other two, Naotsugu was a genuine vanguard warrior, and Warriors had excellent stamina, muscle, and agility scores. Having reached level 90, Naotsugu had enough energy to fight for more than an hour wearing heavy armor that had to weigh forty or fifty kilograms, something that surprised even Naotsugu. Even if he'd completely exhausted himself, his strength would start to return after just a few minutes' rest, and he was confident that he could lift close to three hundred kilograms, provided he didn't have to hold it for long. His strength seemed to be nearly inexhaustible.

Shiroe and Akatsuki were different, though. Shiroe's specialty was intellectual work, and although Akatsuki was astonishingly swift, she was a lightweight fighter who lived by her agility. Both of them said that, since they were level 90, they had quite a lot of stamina, but Naotsugu always felt that it would be better for him to match their pace than expect them to match his... Still, it looked as though he didn't need to worry about that tonight, at least not yet.

They were lucky: The moon was bright, and they had the light from the magic lamp, too. Unlike in the forest, although there was rubble scattered here and there and cracks ran across their path, the once-paved asphalt road sloped gently and was easy to walk on.

"The gobs aren't attacking..."

"And they're not gonna. Not with three level-90 players here."

"I like the ones that wear dinosaur bones on their heads. The way they strut around like they're impressive is funny. Cute, too."

There goes short stuff, talking crazy with that deadpan face of hers...

Akatsuki probably meant the goblin shamans. They were members of the goblin leader class who could attack with flame and ice spells, and they showed up with retinues of low-ranking goblins. It was definitely funny to watch them act like big shots and hand down orders, but Naotsugu could say with utter conviction that they weren't cute.

"You like critters like that, short stuff?" he asked, just to check.

Akatsuki said simply, "They're cute. They die fast, too."

That last bit made sense—they were enemies, after all—but it still didn't explain why she thought they were cute.

"Most magic-user enemies act like they're big and important, but their armor's tissue paper and their HP's practically nonexistent."

Akatsuki answered in a matter-of-fact tone. There was no telling how she'd interpreted Naotsugu's question.

"They really should stay away from the action, but they just swagger right up to the front, so it's easy to take them out. I creep up close using Hide Shadow and spike 'em in the neck with my short sword, and they go all limp and drop like marionettes with cut strings. I love that."

......Whoa. Way to leave Shiro without a leg to stand on, kid.

Naotsugu shot Shiroe a sidelong glance. He'd obviously taken damage from that comment. Everybody knew that all magic users had low Defense, so Naotsugu didn't think it was anything for him to get depressed over. Akatsuki hadn't meant any harm by it.

Even so, Shiroe looked glum, and Akatsuki looked oblivious. Watching the two of them made Naotsugu tired.

Shiro's a smart guy, but he reads too much into things and thinks about stuff too hard... He's a worrywart, that's what he is. I wonder what's got the Counselor so nervous...

To Naotsugu, Shiroe seemed to be holding back. Naotsugu had no idea why he was doing it, but it did feel as if he was. He'd felt that hesitation when they belonged to the Debauchery Tea Party, too. Shiroe was the type who tried to do everything by himself. Lately, that particular trait had started to seem like a rare virtue. Even so, a Guardian's job was to protect the players around him. Not being relied on made him feel as if his job had been taken from him. It was irritating. He wished Shiroe would count on him, even if only for the things he was really good at.

"Well, we magic users can be pretty gutsy when we have to be."

"Hm? You have tissue paper armor, too, my liege... Don't worry about it. I'm your ninja. I'll protect you."

Apparently not noticing that Shiroe was very close to folding, Akatsuki kept sending lethal comments his way. *It's like listening to a couple of kids*, Naotsugu thought, fully aware that Shiroe entertained similar thoughts about him most of the time.

Except for the absurd dialogue, overall it was a quiet night. They did see the long shadows of skulking goblins, but whenever Naotsugu and the others turned their way, the goblins panicked and ran.

"It's because this is the zone right next to Akiba," Shiroe said. "High-level monsters don't show up here. If they did, new players would die all over the place."

It had been more than ten days since they got pulled into this world, and in that time, not a single new player had appeared. What was happening to their real-world versions? Had their entire group vanished off the face of the earth? Were they comatose vegetables? They didn't know.

...This is one of those ideas, but what if "we're" all actually still there, right where we're supposed to be, living like we usually do?... Whoa. If that's true, we'll have no place to go back to. A blowout sale on absolutely-nobody-needs-us going on right now. Or what if it's like one of those books, and as far as the real world's concerned, we never existed at all? Like we were never born or something. That would bum me out, too.

Not that you'd know it to look at him, but as his thoughts showed, Naotsugu read fantasy novels. However, at this point in time, there was no way for them to check any of those theories.

It might have been "just ten days," and it might have been "ten days already." No doubt opinions on that score varied wildly from person to person, but gradually, whether they liked it or not, Naotsugu, Shiroe, and Akatsuki were getting used to this world.

Even though it was contorted by two sets of restrictions—the *Elder Tales* specs and the physical laws of some other world—this world did have its own rules. This was true even of unrealistic phenomena, such as the fact that all food, without exception, tasted like soggy rice crackers. Yes, lots of things were unreasonable, and they frequently felt irritated by the unreasonableness. Even so, there was nothing for it but to understand those rules and live within their limits. That was what it meant to belong to a world, whether that world was a game world or the real one.

Since we don't have any idea how to get back home, I guess the world we're standing in is the only one there is, and it doesn't matter whether it used to be a game or not... Still, it's actually not bad. Swinging a sword around, adventuring... Once you get used to 'em, they're not bad... I bluffed and told Miss Mari that things weren't half as bad as they could be, but maybe I said that because I'm the one who really wanted to hear it.

A big part of Naotsugu was already starting to adapt to this life, and that was all for the best. He hadn't had any complaints about the real world, not at all, but if asked whether he'd sell off a chunk of his soul to get back, he'd have to confess that he didn't really know.

It's not like I had a girlfriend who'd show me her panties, and I haven't seen my folks in almost two years... I'd gotten used to my job, but did it really feel like a job worth doing? ...Well, no.

While he was absently thinking about this and that, they'd crossed from Ichigaya into Kudanshita, and now they were just two gates away from Akiba. This time, they were planning to head into Akiba from the top of the Ochanomizu hill, without cutting through the Forest of Library Towers zone. The slope that led to the Roka Charity Hospital was a gentle incline that stirred faint feelings of nostalgia. From the Japanese garden on the right of the road, broadleaf trees stretched branches shaggy with leaves out over the road like open overcoats.

The moon was visible through the fragmented gaps in the overcoats, between the leaves, and it went into shadow several times.

Abruptly, Naotsugu and the others scattered in all directions, putting distance between themselves and the shifting flecks of moonlight on the road.

——!!

Naotsugu was in the middle of a step forward, and without slowing, he struck at the darkness in front of him with the shield he still wore on his left arm. A cry of pain rose from the shadows. Naotsugu sensed Shiroe a dozen meters behind him, backing away. He concentrated on the presences he could sense in front of him, careful to pay attention to his surroundings as he did so.

That's one, two... Three? Four of them?

This wasn't a situation they hadn't anticipated, but now that it was actually happening, his mouth had gone dry. The tension he felt when battling monsters was nothing compared to this.

All of a sudden, there was a low, steady sound, as if someone was dragging a bundle of metal.

Gkh! I'm not gonna make it!!

Without stopping to check behind him, Naotsugu tried to jump back, but a chain reared up like a snake and coiled around his ankles. It wasn't a completely physical metal chain. It was a magic-generated semisolid binding spell.

Naotsugu had been thrown off-balance in midair, and the spell rendered him completely unable to move. A colorless, soundless ripple of magic surged up from behind him. Dispel Magic. One of Shiroe's spells. The magic dissolution spell destroyed the magical chain that had slithered up from beneath his feet.

Excellent reaction support, as usual. Okay, Counselor! What now?!

Exhilaration and the urge to fight were welling up inside him. The confidence that he'd be able to protect Shiroe, and that Shiroe would have his back, filled him with energy.

"Naotsugu, series formation! They're PKs; four visually confirmed. I'll pin down their locations. —There!!"

Shiroe yelled on the moonlit road in the dead of night. As he did so, a magic arrow flew from his staff in a burst of pale light. Mind Bolt was one of the Enchanters' basic attack spells, one that targeted a single enemy and inflicted a set amount of damage. The damage was far less than what a Summoner or Sorcerer of the same level could inflict, but the spell saw frequent use as a basic Enchanter self-defense spell. Shiroe always lamented his spells' lack of power, but Naotsugu had never once seen it as a problem. A well-timed small spell was much more effective than a huge spell that missed its target.

"Enemy sighted!"

Shiroe's spell had given Naotsugu exactly what he wanted this time, too. Although it was only for a fraction of a second, the pale fox fire glow illuminated the PKs lurking in the shadows as it streaked through the darkness. Obeying Shiroe's instructions, Naotsugu quickly put some distance between him and the darkness in front of him, ending up about halfway between the darkness and Shiroe. He was right in the center of the two-lane road.

Naotsugu could have charged the enemies he'd spotted in the darkness. However, for now, he backed up and regrouped. In a series formation, the distance between him and the end of the line was important. Too much distance, and the end's shaky defense would leave it wide open.

"There's guts for you. PKs... Huhn." Naotsugu spat out the feelings seething inside him. "Gone straight to acting like animals 'cos you miss your mama? A surprise attack isn't enough to warrant a victory party, guys."

The opponents he was facing weren't monsters. They were players who liked doing the sort of thing Naotsugu hated most.

PK stood for "player kill" or "player killer." It could mean either the act of attacking and killing other players instead of monsters or a player who did such things.

The town of Akiba was a designated noncombat zone, but the fact that combat was expressly banned in some zones meant it was perfectly okay in others. The administrators of *Elder Tales* allowed fights between players. However, due to a number of in-game factors—for example, the low success rate of PKs, the high risk, and cultural issues on the Japanese server (even online, Japanese people were orderly and disliked violence between players)—had meant that player killing wasn't a very popular act.

One of the reasons for the low PK success rate in *Elder Tales* had been the existence of a mini-map that displayed on the screen and showed all the beings in the immediate area, including players, monsters, and non-player characters.

Another was that high-level characters would automatically avoid attacks launched at them using any method that matched their skill set, whether or not the player did anything. In other words, surprise attacks weren't very effective. On top of that, although player killing wasn't banned in *Elder Tales*, harassment was. PK wasn't harassment in and of itself, but there were cases in which killing the same person over and over or verbally abusing an opponent had been considered harassment, and harassment carried a high probability of getting slapped with a warning or penalty by the game corporation.

In addition, the standards for whether or not something constituted harassment were pretty vague and subjective. Although player killing was technically legal, in a few cases where the victim had been female, it had been judged harassment and the problem user's account had been abruptly suspended.

Due to all those reasons, player killing was considered very risky.

Now that they'd been pulled into this other world, though, things were different. During battles here, that mini-map didn't exist, not even on the mental menu. No matter how high an Adventurer's level was, if they didn't see the attack coming, the auto-evade function wouldn't activate. Unless the actual player was a martial arts expert, they probably wouldn't be able to stay constantly on the alert.

On top of that, decisions regarding harassment had been made by a supervisor at the game corporation who went through the play logs and dealt with incidents after the fact. When *Elder Tales* was a game, order had been maintained by this corporate "hand of God." However, in this world, that convenient salvation didn't exist.

Surprise attacks were far more likely to succeed. The risk of an incident being reported as harassment was low. On top of that, player killing was a very tempting proposition. Since PKs could take all the money a defeated player had been carrying and several of their items, the rewards were much greater than anything they could win in a battle with monsters. Some items would always belong to their bearer and couldn't be reassigned, but about half of the normal, tradable items in players' packs would be scattered around the immediate area the instant the player died.

The advantages and disadvantages had been flipped, and in the current *Elder Tales*, player killing was on the rise.

▶ 3

Well, we lasted through the surprise attack anyway..., Shiroe thought, holding the staff he'd infused with fox fire. *The other side has a terrain advantage and the advantage of numbers, and they've gone over their game plan beforehand. They're ready for this. Our advantages, on the other hand...*

He ran through the spell icons he could use. He'd registered all the spells he used regularly in shortcut slots so that he wouldn't have to locate them on the mental menu screen with the cursor. They were right there, ready to use. However, before Shiroe had time to level his staff and prepare to chant, several players appeared from the darkness of the ruin ahead of them.

The bone-dry asphalt crumbled, sending a weirdly loud sound through the quiet night.

Four shadows had appeared. One Warrior type. Two brigand types. One healer. Four was a lot, and from the confident way they walked, he guessed their levels weren't low.

"Drop your packs and leave quietly, and we'll let you live."

The Warrior delivered the usual line in a condescending voice.

The words drew a wry smile from Shiroe.

Sounds like somebody's been reading too much manga.

Although they'd grown fairly used to monster battles, battling players would be completely different. Unlike monsters, which were guided by their animal instincts, there was no telling what a human enemy would do. That was scary enough, but on top of that, the malice behind the attacks was impossible to tune out. Monsters sometimes projected intent to kill, but PKs hit you with an intent to plunder.

Their malice was the type that wanted to make an easy profit from other players' work.

Shiroe's palms had grown slick with clammy sweat. He was actually grateful to the guy in front of him for perpetrating that clichéd line and easing the tension.

"A Guardian and a magic user, huh? Resistance is futile, but feel free to try. As you can see, it's two against four."

The bandit who'd spoken seemed to be in charge of the group. The two longswords that hung at his hips marked him as a Swashbuckler. Of the twelve classes, only Swashbucklers and Samurai were able to fight with two swords without using any special equipment or work-arounds.

"What do you want to do, Naotsugu?"

"Kill 'em. I'll fillet 'em, then grind 'em into hamburger. These guys murder people for fun, so you know they've been prepared to get offed by some other guy since they were in diapers."

Naotsugu's voice was steady, and Shiroe felt the strength start to return to his knees.

Breathing normal, sense of balance okay... I'm calm. I can do this. I thought something like this might happen someday. We'd have had to do this eventually, he told himself.

He was ready to fight. Still, if possible, he wanted to drag the conversation out a little longer.

"Naotsugu hates PKs, you see... As far as I'm concerned, I wouldn't mind paying you, as long as it's just this once."

At Shiroe's words, the men smirked. Still smirking, they took half a step forward, making the ugly threat glaringly obvious. Even though he knew what was going on, the pressure was so great that Shiroe wanted to look away.

...In other words, they're underestimating me. They think I'll pay up if they threaten me.

He felt himself splitting into two Shiroes: one whose legs were about to give out on him and one whose mind was oddly clear. At the same time, he felt a hot pulse begin near his ears. It was a sensation he'd felt many times during his Debauchery Tea Party days.

Shiroe wasn't good with Akatsuki, but that didn't mean he didn't like her.

Shiroe didn't like fighting, but that didn't mean he wasn't good at it.

"...Unfortunately, though, I don't want to pay you jerks."

"Attaboy, Shiro."

Maybe they hadn't expected Shiroe and Naotsugu's interchange, or maybe it had irritated them. Either way, the bandits' faces flushed red. Spitting curses, they all drew their weapons at once.

The "Battle" icon had been blinking ever since the surprise attack, and its border was so red it seemed to stain his eyelids. Shiroe took half a step back with his left foot and, praying that his voice would come out as calmly as possible, began issuing orders.

"The first target is the left-front Warrior! Hold them back, too."

"We'll handle the armor-plated Warrior! You go put down the magic user!!"

The bandit leader's yell came at almost the same time as Shiroe's tactical instructions.

Naotsugu took one sharp step in and swung his phosphorescent shield at the Warrior in front of him. The man held a katana, which meant he was probably a Samurai. The long-haired thief that the bandit leader's orders had singled out slipped past Naotsugu and lunged for Shiroe, but it was just one of the moves Shiroe had anticipated, and in the next instant, the man had been hit by one of Shiroe's spells.

Astral Bind was a movement restriction spell, like the one that had trapped Naotsugu earlier. Magic users had problematic Defense, so when they adventured alone, one of their basic combat tactics was to use this sort of spell to slow down monsters, then finish them off from a distance with attack spells. Although the details differed, the three magic-user classes used spells with the same fundamental properties. It was a basic spell that simply restricted movement.

That said, restricting movement was all it did.

The long-haired bandit did an about-face. Then, seeming resigned to the situation, he joined the attack on Naotsugu, brandishing a knife so big it was practically a small sword. The movement restriction spell only prevented long-distance movement; it didn't paralyze the target. It was a little like tying a dog to a telephone pole with a chain several meters long, and it didn't restrict movement within that range. It wouldn't even last very long.

"Switch! You do it!"

"I'm on it!"

Lit by sparks from the clashing swords, the bandit leader feinted nimbly and tried to get past Naotsugu. His first strategy had apparently been to join the bandit warrior in attacking Naotsugu and to have his underling kill Shiroe. As soon as he'd seen his underling was hobbled, he'd switched roles and was planning to take Shiroe out himself. He'd abandoned his previous formation and immediately reworked it to suit present conditions. The speed of the decision was admirable. The feint attack and the speed with which he turned also passed muster.

—*He can't beat Naotsugu's experience, though.*

"Anchor Howl!!"

Naotsugu dropped into a crouch and gave a piercing yell. The roar, which seemed to shake the air, was a Guardian technique. The bandit leader who'd been about to slip past Naotsugu cringed back reflexively as if he'd touched a superheated prominence, then froze up with his twin swords still pointed at Naotsugu. His knees had gone watery; he seemed unable to tear his eyes away from Naotsugu, and he was dripping with a nasty sort of greasy sweat.

The same thing was happening to the Samurai and the long-haired bandit: Their eyes were wide, and all three seemed to be choking back terror. If any of them took his eyes off Naotsugu now, he'd be killed in a single attack. That was the terror the three men who surrounded Naotsugu were struggling against.

As a Guardian, Naotsugu's job was to protect his companions. Guardians were commonly known as "tanks," because they acted as shields to block enemy attacks. Still, just being durable with high HP wasn't enough to make a good tank. Some monsters, such as goblins and orcs, were as intelligent as humans. In the world of *Elder Tales*, Adventurers could find themselves fighting ancient magical weapons, dark elves, or the adherents of heretical religions. It was common for enemies to avoid the tank, which was designed to take attacks, and go after the healer or magic user at the rear of the party instead.

Since Guardians were specialized to protect their companions from countless enemies that could use all sorts of strategies, they'd never conclude that just being tough and having good HP was enough to get the job done. Anchor Howl was a special technique that made use of the Guardian's piercing shout. Any enemy who heard this yell was rendered unable to ignore Naotsugu. The instant they tried, Naotsugu would hit them with a ferocious counterattack right when they were at their most defenseless. It was a Guardian special technique that launched an attack if an enemy let their guard down even slightly. This technique, which drew all enemy attacks to itself, was the reason Guardians were known as the toughest of the Warrior classes.

"Tch! Ignore it! There's three of us and one of him. He may be tough, but he ain't *that* tough. We'll get rid of this guy first!"

Still unsettled by his terror, the bandit leader spurred on his underlings. Forced to change tactics once again, the Swashbuckler had decided to target Naotsugu. His twin blades wove like snakes, searching for a chink in Naotsugu's Defense. He'd decided to overcome Naotsugu with the bandit Samurai, his own twin blades, and the long-haired brigand.

It wasn't a bad approach.

"Dammit! You don't scare me! Defense is the only move you've got!"

The man screamed hysterically, launching a rapid series of attacks.

"Your sword moves are never gonna break my guard!"

Naotsugu sounded almost cheerful, and it made the bandits even more ferocious.

As he listened to the metallic echoes of steel on steel from the rear, Shiroe quickly checked Naotsugu's status. These player killers did have guts and good teamwork. Their continuous attacks were whittling down Naotsugu's HP. In thirty seconds, even Naotsugu would fall.

If they manage to keep it up for thirty seconds, that is, Shiroe thought.

The corners of his lips curved slightly. *We're not naive enough to give them that time.*

It took 1.5 seconds flat to draw six runes with the tip of his staff. Shiroe launched the resulting crackling ball of electricity at the enemy Samurai. The sphere was a continuous attack spell known as Electrical Fuzz. It didn't do much damage, but it would zap the enemy with sporadic electric shocks for ten to twenty seconds.

"Hah! What're you, an Enchanter? What's with this wussy spell?! You couldn't kill a *dog* with that damage!!"

The Samurai who'd taken Shiroe's attack did look a bit annoyed, but he snorted, laughing off the spell. The tennis ball–sized lightning sphere that was following him around did make quite a racket, but for the most part it only gave off beautiful, crackling light, and it caused no pain to speak of.

Overall, Enchanter attack spells tended not to cause much damage, and continuous spells like this one spread that slight damage out over the length of the spell. In terms of total damage, it did outperform Mind Bolt, but the damage per second was far lower. The fact that the sensation was more itchy than painful showed how low the damage really was. As far as the Samurai was concerned, it was no more than a nuisance.

"Weak" is right… But even so.

Shiroe had heard taunts like that many times before. He was well aware of the properties of his spells. Instead of responding to the taunt, he launched two more Electrical Fuzz spells, hitting the leader and the long-haired bandit. The two Weapon Attack classes had slightly lower HP than the Warrior Samurai, but as before, the spell and its paltry damage didn't faze either of them.

"Ha-ha-ha-ha! What are you trying to pull back there? Or what, are you some newbie that's been trailing this big guy around?!"

The three PKs redoubled their attacks on Naotsugu, and the orbiting spells shone like power lines that showered pale sparks or like grotesque fireworks that lit up the night.

…All right. Let's take one down.

The bandits' anger. Their carelessness. Their scorn. Shiroe took all these things in as information, condensing them in one breath. Then, with flawless timing, he took two steps forward. He swung his staff sharply, chanting a spell aloud, and called up a shortcut. The two-second chant generated a Sewn-Bind Hostage spell. Shining sapphire rings flew at the Samurai, wrapping around him like five brambles.

"What the heck?! Gkh!"

Naotsugu swung his sword as if to destroy the brambles, and a light like a burst flashbulb lit up the darkness. At the shock wave, the Samurai screamed and reflexively cringed back.

Sewn-Bind Hostage was an attack spell that Shiroe used regularly. Unlike single-shot attack spells and range-scorching spells, the activation conditions were complex, and the spell had to be "set" on the targeted opponent beforehand. Once the shining bramble restraints had been set, when the magic user's companion hit the target with a physical attack, the attack gained an additional one thousand damage points. The number of brambles and the amount of damage varied by spell rank, but Shiroe's Sewn-Bind Hostage was a secret-class spell. Even if the player was a Warrior, if all five brambles burst, that alone would be enough to wipe out half their HP.

"Calm down! It's a damn set spell. Get rid of it, healer!! Concentrate your recovery on the Samurai! We've got double their numbers! We can't lose!!"

Unlike the Samurai, who'd actually taken damage and was panicking, the leader's voice was still fairly calm.

Healers in *Elder Tales* were fairly powerful entities. A single healer with decent skills was able to use recovery spells that could nearly cancel out the damage from an enemy on the same level as the player or from several players. Even if Shiroe's Sewn-Bind Hostage was powerful, as long as the recovery spell continued uninterrupted, the Samurai had nothing to worry about. The leader of this PK group had strategies that could handle even a Sorcerer's powerful attack spells, let alone an Enchanter's puny ones. His confidence wasn't empty bravado.

Naotsugu's sword flashed. Each strike triggered the bramble trap and sent a shock wave of damage through the Samurai. The Samurai was trying to pull himself together, but each time he got a better grip on his katana, the slashes and shock waves from both sides made a mockery of his efforts.

"Hah! So what?! Your flank's wide open!"

The long-haired bandit jammed his huge knife—a type of woodsman's knife—into Naotsugu's right side. Naotsugu had just hit the end of a sword swing; he wasn't able to completely dodge the blow and was wounded through a chink in his armor.

"Looks like havin' a healer is gonna win us the battle! That's what you get for underestimating us, dweebs! Bwah-ha-ha-ha-ha-ha! Go have a good cry over it at the temple!"

Reinforced with Shiroe's weapon-strengthening spell, Naotsugu's attacks had been more than sharp enough for the Warrior, and Shiroe's secret-level spell had caused great damage for an Enchanter. Even so, though, recovery performed by a healer on their level was a formidable

defense, and they stood very little chance of breaking through it. The leader's roar of laughter was backed by this confidence.

"You have a good grasp of the situation, yes."

"Yeah. *If* your healer's doing his job!!"

Like lightning, Naotsugu dropped into a crouch so deep it was as if he'd lost half his height, then slashed right through the Samurai's knees. The attack was like one clean sweep of a giant praying mantis's arm, and still upright, the Samurai dropped like a stone. It was an oddly quiet end: no soaring, limp body, no gouts of blood. At the sudden change in the Samurai, who'd been ferociously attacking with his katana just a moment ago, the leader abruptly stopped laughing.

"—Wh-what?! What did you do?!"

The leader was ranting.

"Is it paralysis? Hey, healer!! What are you doing?! Hurry up and heal him!!"

Naotsugu took a one-handed swing at the leader, putting all his strength behind it.

"Shut *up,* dude. It's a beautiful night. Quit polluting it with bad two-bit punk lines!"

"Wha—?! Wha—?!"

That took less time than I thought it would—full marks for professionalism.

Shiroe shot a glance into the trees in the garden on his right. From the road, flooded as it was with blue-white light from multiple spells, the darkness of the thickly wooded garden was completely impenetrable.

However, Shiroe knew he had a companion somewhere in that darkness.

"Dammit! Enough already! Hey, Sorceror! Summoner! It's time for a full-on war! Incinerate this guy!"

The bandit leader seemed to have finally decided to play the trump card he'd been hiding and call in his reserves.

So he had two magic users. He's right: With two more members, they could still kill us by inches, even now. They've taken damage, but it was just one Samurai. There are two of us and five of them. They've got more than twice our power. "We can't possibly lose," hm?

Shiroe could guess what the leader was thinking. However, even the fact that he'd had reserve troops waiting wasn't a surprise to Shiroe.

They hit Naotsugu with a binding movement prevention spell, but the only members who showed themselves were a Warrior, two brigands, and a healer. No magic users. He tipped his hand right there.

To Shiroe, it had been obvious from the beginning that the PK group had at least one magic user, and he'd incorporated the fact that they'd be waiting in ambush in the thickly wooded garden on his right into his plan.

They left magic users, with low HP and thin armor, on their own, unguarded. That means...

"C'mon, hurry up! Get this guy!!"

The bandit leader screamed, but he was backing away as he did so. Although he pointed at Naotsugu with the sword he held in his right hand, the point of the sword was more than a meter away from Naotsugu. Shiroe and Naotsugu's fighting methods and the sheer uncanniness of the situation seemed to have drained his morale.

"It looks like we win."

"Correct, my liege."

A small shadow welled up from between the trees. Akatsuki, wearing her usual too-serious expression, flung the two magic users she'd been dragging onto the road. The sight of a beautiful, slight, black-haired girl who couldn't have been 150 centimeters tall tossing his companions around like sacks of garbage completely boggled the bandit leader.

"Wha— Wha—?! What are you two doing?! Wh-why didn't you report in?! Huh— Healer!! I told you a million times to keep track of our HP! You little—Did you sell us out...?"

"This is exactly what makes you so lame."

The bandit's words seemed to have been the last straw for Naotsugu: He swung at him with the shield on his left arm. The Swashbuckler staggered at the sudden attack and sat down with a thump in the middle of the road.

"You should trust your companions, at least. Your healer is just sleeping. He's been asleep since the beginning of the battle."

Shiroe's merciless declaration echoed over the road.

Astral Hypno was the Enchanter's ultimate binding spell, one that supported him and simultaneously strengthened his allies. The very existence of anything targeted with this suspension spell was plunged into deep slumber. Its effect didn't last long. Even extended, it lasted a mere dozen seconds. Not only that, but if the target was attacked, the spell would be broken instantly. In a sense, it was a fool's spell, useful only for buying time.

Fundamentally, battles were contests in which each party tried to steal the other's ability to fight. To put it bluntly, the goal was to kill each other. Just putting the enemy to sleep could never be enough to win a battle. It was a spell that didn't directly contribute to ending the fight.

Enchanters were considered to be a cut below for that very reason.

"Don't make fun of my liege's spells."

"—!"

While they'd been distracted, silence had returned to the road. The balls of electricity had been sparking up until a few seconds ago, but the effect time had run out for all of them and they'd vanished. In the road were the two brigands, whose legs had given out; one healer, fast asleep; and Shiroe, Naotsugu, and Akatsuki, looking down at them.

"I hear you made fun of the electrical fireworks because they didn't do any damage. If your field of vision was full of bright, sparking things, you'd never be able to see into the darkness of the forest. You didn't even notice that the healer who was supposed to be supporting you from the background was asleep. Your teamwork is full of holes. You were so absorbed in fighting that you forgot to keep track of your HP or check your companions' statuses. It made it easy to assassinate your reserves."

Naotsugu raised his longsword, as if he couldn't wait for Akatsuki to finish speaking. One swing and the long-haired bandit, who'd lost all will to fight, died with a piercing shriek.

"E-even if you kill us, we'll come right back. We didn't lose to you!"

The bandit leader blustered, but with Akatsuki's short sword pressed to his neck, he couldn't even move.

Akatsuki glanced at Shiroe, a question in her eyes.

She was asking for permission to kill.

Shiroe heaved a deep sigh. If they'd wanted to, it wouldn't have been out of the question for them to tie the man up, torture him, and take everything he had, but Shiroe really wasn't a fan of torture. He doubted he'd be able to actually go through with it.

We could just let him walk, of course. But even if we did...

The guy probably wouldn't thank them for it. He was even more unlikely to give up and never PK again. He'd feel as if he'd been insulted and resent them for it. In any case, in this world where death was a mere shell of itself, it was doubtful whether crime or punishment worked the same way as they had in their old world. Even Shiroe knew that.

Still, did that mean "anything goes"? Shiroe was pretty sure it didn't.

I guess there's no help for it.

Shiroe gave Akatsuki a nod. With no hesitation, she plunged her sharp short sword into the PK leader's neck. Blood spurted out, red even in the dark, but turbid and cloudy. As Akatsuki nimbly side-stepped the blood, the fallen leader's items and money scattered across the area.

With that, the PK attack was truly over.

▶ **4**

"People said things had gotten rougher. I guess it's true."

Naotsugu mused as he picked up items. Shiroe shrugged. In front of the bandits, he'd pretended that they'd had everything under control, but as a matter of fact, it hadn't been an easy win. There had been six enemies, and most of them had certainly been fairly high level, if not actually level 90. Naotsugu had been using special Defense techniques, and even he'd lost nearly half his HP. What if Akatsuki hadn't quickly dispatched the members waiting in the shadows? Or even earlier: What if she hadn't promptly taken cover or understood what Shiroe really meant when he said "four visually confirmed" and gone to work as a commando unit of one? The battle could easily have gone the other way.

Of course, both Naotsugu and Shiroe kept a card or two up their sleeves. Probably Akatsuki did as well. Still, although such cards were a way to turn the tables in a fight, using them required a cool head. A panicked player would have serious trouble turning the tide, even with a brilliant trump card. In order to play a card like that, you needed to have a chance at winning—in other words, a cool head and a plan. They'd won this time because the bandits had put too much faith in the strength of their numbers and because Shiroe's group had better teamwork.

"I wonder if there are any more PKs lurking around here."

Akatsuki cocked her head slightly to one side, looking up at the cluster of abandoned buildings.

"I shouldn't think so," Shiroe answered.

In player kills, surprise attacks were everything, and they needed to be launched from suitable locations. Any closer to Akiba, and victims might escape into the city. That would be too much of a handicap for the PKs.

...Although we'd better not let our guard down. Things really are getting dangerous.

There was one more reason they'd been able to beat back the PKs, Shiroe thought: the information that public order was deteriorating. They'd heard rumors that player kills were occurring more frequently. The PKs would launch surprise attacks in the field zones around Akiba, waiting until it was dark and visibility was bad. The group they'd just fought hadn't seemed new at this. Their skills had obviously been seasoned to the point where they could easily be overconfident.

Shiroe and the others had proceeded with caution in large part because they'd heard that rumor, and their caution was the reason they'd noticed the shadows watching them from the treetops.

"Dread Pack, huh...? I dunno, guys. That's a pretty generic name," Naotsugu muttered, spitting out the words and making no attempt to hide his disgust. He'd found the guild name in their personal information. Dread Pack.

"There's no help for that. You can't expect good taste from a guild that PKs."

Akatsuki sympathized with Naotsugu.

Well, I'm mad, too.

Shiroe sighed.

Naotsugu hated PKs. So did Shiroe, for that matter.

There were several reasons. However, Shiroe suspected that all those reasons were afterthoughts, and that, deep down, it was very simple. The heart of the matter was that most PKs were seriously uncool.

To Shiroe's mind, the mere idea of swiping items and coins that other players had worked hard to get was uncool all by itself. Even less cool was that coins and items gained that way would never get one to the top.

Taking treasure that other people had worked for meant that the thieves never set foot in the difficult zones where that treasure could be won. That meant they couldn't stumble onto undiscovered places or solve mysteries and they'd never find items that no one had ever seen before. As a play method, player killing would never let you stand on the front line of an adventure.

PKs were incompetents who couldn't do anything but steal other people's achievements, and they'd never be anything more than parasites.

That was what Shiroe thought of them anyway.

Talking about "cool" and "uncool" may mean nothing to the players who've been trapped here, though... Maybe there's no help for that. We're all living pretty close to the edge mentally.

Unfortunately, that state of living close to the edge was fast becoming the accepted norm.

"I've heard that rumor, too," Akatsuki murmured.

"From what I hear, Tidal Clan, Blue Impact, and Canossa are killing players, too," Shiroe told her.

"I dunno. It's just... Between this and that, I know everyone's pretty close to snapping. I know. *But.* How do I put this... Don't they have anything better to do?"

"Like...?"

"Wax philosophical about panties and stuff."

Akatsuki took an obvious step away from Naotsugu. Then she peered around the area and took another step back.

"She took two steps back on me... *Two!*"

Naotsugu sounded glum. Shiroe thumped him lightly on the shoulder to cheer him up. With a desperate expression on his face, Naotsugu attempted to launch into a speech about how marvelous panty fetishes were, but at Akatsuki's "Quiet, sex fiend," he fell silent.

Their party's power dynamics were rapidly becoming established.

Something better to do...

The fact that there was nothing was a problem in their present situation. If all one needed to do was keep themselves alive, there was cheap food available. True, it tasted like soggy rice crackers with absolutely no salt, but it would keep a person alive, so they couldn't complain too loudly. Their situation was nowhere near as bad as it had been in some areas of their old world, in Southeast Asia or in war zones, where whole countries were gasping for food and children's hunger showed in their glittering eyes as they starved to death. It was also likely that it would never be that bad in the future.

In the world of *Elder Tales*, food items were made by combining several ingredient items, and ingredient items could be gathered in the field zones. Meat could be taken from monsters killed in battle, mushrooms and edible wild plants could be gathered, marine products could be caught, grain could be grown, and fruit could be picked from fruit trees. It was still too soon to tell whether the concept of seasons existed in this world, but at the very least, it had in *Elder Tales*. From the feel of the air, it was currently early summer. The fields were overflowing with ingredients. In that case, even newbie players who hadn't hit level 10 yet would be able to find ingredient items in the comparatively safe fields near Akiba.

A bigger issue was whether the players with Chef subclasses—and there weren't many—would turn those ingredient items into food. From what Shiroe had heard, though, lots of players had changed their subclasses to Chef over the past ten days. Since absorbing nutrients was one of the basic requirements for life, it was a pretty good strategy.

The same went for clothes. Hides could be taken from animals, and hemp and silk could be used to make cloth. If one wasn't picky about the statistical performance of their equipment, a production-class artisan could make a set of clothes in ten seconds or so. Shoes and almost all daily necessities could be obtained from Tailors, Blacksmiths, and Woodworkers. Carpenters handled larger items, while Artificers created delicate jewelry and mechanisms.

It was easy to find housing: As long as a person didn't care too much about safety or comfort, one could spend the night in any abandoned building. It cost about five gold coins to rent cheap lodging, an amount even a level-10 player could get by defeating a few goblins. If a player wanted more, of course, they could rent comfortable lodging by the month or find a place at a guildhall with a group or even own a house, but if they were content with just having a place to sleep, there were any number of simple ways to get it.

…All of which meant that, in this other world, there was no need to risk one's life or work long hours if surviving was the only item on their agenda. As far as "survival" was concerned, conditions would never be that miserable.

Although, if you asked me whether that was "living," I'd say it was more like just not being dead…

To Shiroe, this lack of having to struggle to survive was linked to having lost all purpose in life. People were left with "nothing better to do."

Of course, in this world, they were free.

They almost seemed to be a bit *too* free. Naotsugu would probably say, "A purpose in life? Something better to do? Just figure that out for yourself and get to work. You could talk about cute girls or protect cute girls or…" He'd be right, and Shiroe had no intention of arguing with him.

However, there were people who could say that and people who couldn't. In addition, the sort of people who were drawn to gloomy thoughts because they hadn't managed to find something they could devote themselves to could be found anywhere. The sort of people who convinced themselves they were big and powerful by tormenting other people, for example.

It's the same with PKs. There are lots of far easier, safer ways to survive here. Anyway, you don't need a lot of money just to live. There's no need to kill players just to get money.

Even if there had been, player killing would never work as a survival strategy. It was completely different from the sort of thing that happened in extremely impoverished countries, where people were forced to turn to robbery just to survive.

To these guys, player killing *was* their "something better to do." A way to feel fulfilled, something separate from just surviving. It struck Shiroe as incredibly uncool somehow.

"Hey, what the—?!" Naotsugu yelled.

"What's the matter?"

"These guys only had sixty-two gold coins. Total. How sorry is that?!"

Akatsuki and Naotsugu had finished checking through the items they'd picked up, and it sounded as though the financial haul had been disappointing.

"They had some decent items, though."

"Well, sure. They were PKs. They knew it was risky," Shiroe pointed out. "Unless they're complete idiots, they probably left everything except the bare necessities in a safe-deposit box. The items they had were probably stolen from some other player."

The other two sighed heavily, grumbling about wasted effort.

▶ 5

It was the middle of the night by the time they got back to Akiba.

Lately, the streets seemed to be seething with menace. Rows of stalls still stood in the center of town—in the plaza in front of the station, for example, or the great intersection or at Akiba Bridge—and they still drew a fair number of customers, but on the shadow-filled outskirts of town or in tangled alleyways crowded with abandoned buildings, wary players kept their distance from strangers and went about their business without speaking to anyone.

Order really is beginning to break down…

For the past several days, this one included, Shiroe and the others had been out in the field zones, battling. In the few days following the disaster, sharing information in town had been very meaningful, because there had been all sorts of things that they'd needed to confirm: information on food and places to sleep and basic information about the world's structure and specs. Once they had that basic information, though, Shiroe's group had elected to gather information on the field zones and discover what had changed about battles. It was a decision they'd made together after talking things over, but the hunt for information was taking longer than they'd expected. There was a huge gap between using spells and techniques and using them *well*.

was fated to be forcibly sent to their place of execution, several hundred meters below.

Shiroe and his group, who'd avoided that trap and were lurking as quietly as they could on the ground, had four options: (1) They could take a big detour to the ocean; (2) they could trek through the dense forest that covered the Tearstone Mountains, crossing the range that way; (3) they could cut through the Depths of Palm, a complex of ancient tunnels and mineshafts that ran deep under the Tearstone Mountains.; or (4) they could go up the roads that ran through the mountains. After some discussion, Shiroe and the others decided to go through the tunnels. All things considered, that route would take the least amount of time, and it seemed to be the safest course.

Fifteen hours ago, they'd entered the tunnels through the ruins of an enormous ancient construction site cut into the rock face in the forested foothills of the mountain. Instead of the rough dirt-walled cavern they'd expected, the tunnel proved to be a vast underground passage with pale gray concrete walls that ran on and on in the glow of their Magic Light. Like the main drainage tunnel of an underground water treatment plant, the passage was interrupted at regular intervals by narrow branch tunnels to the right and left, and sometimes they passed dull, boxy rooms whose original purpose was a complete mystery.

The intent of the space's designer and any traces of its users had been eroded over the aeons, until now they lay buried under the dust and the rubble. The current owners of this enormous cavern and its underground streams were the ratmen.

Among the many species of demihumans that populated this world, ratmen were a fairly low-ranking variety. As far as appearance went, they looked like something halfway between a human with a rat's head and a rat standing on its hind legs. They were about as tall as a middle schooler, but the smooth, damp-looking fur that covered them from head to toe made it difficult to see what their bodies were shaped like. They could use simple tools, but to high-level players like Shiroe and the others, their combat abilities were no threat whatsoever. Although it depended on the individual, ratmen tended to be even weaker than goblins or orcs.

That said, they still had two troublesome weapons: numbers and plague. True to the phrase "to multiply like rats," normal rats were astoundingly vigorous breeders. Possibly the ratmen were as well, because considerable numbers of them tended to live concentrated in small areas. Since entering the tunnel, in fact, on several occasions, Shiroe and the others had seen more than twenty ratmen huddled in rooms a few meters square.

Under normal circumstances, any creature that sensed the approach of something much stronger would run the other way. This reaction was particularly marked in wild animals, and the ratmen were no exception. Shiroe, Naotsugu, and Akatsuki were high-level players, and the monsters around them seemed to sense it. As proof, throughout the journey from Akiba to this tunnel, Shiroe and the others hadn't fought any battles to speak of. They were on a mission to rescue Serara, and so they'd come this far without pausing for anything, avoiding unnecessary combat training or exploration. If the monsters ran away from them, it was all for the best.

Still, if they were dealing with large, concentrated groups of monsters like the ratmen, and if they happened to stumble onto a group in an enclosed room or a narrow dead end, things would be very different. Even if the ratmen tried to run, they'd have nowhere to go. In that case, even if Shiroe's group tried to retreat and give them their space, they'd most likely attack in a frenzy. It would be a real-life case of the cornered rat biting the cat. Shiroe didn't think they'd lose in combat, but it would take time to defeat so many ratmen, and it wouldn't do their nerves any good.

The other issue was plague. Like medieval rats, ratmen were carriers of the plague. If the *Elder Tales* specs had been faithfully reproduced here as well, the plague was a nasty one that would inhibit recovery and cause continuous damage.

The ratmen in this tunnel were all around level 40. Transmitted plagues had levels as well, and the levels were linked to the host. In this case, the plague would have to be around level 40 as well. A mid-level healer could have treated it easily, but Shiroe's group didn't have a healer. They were drinking the Antibacterial Potions they'd bought at the market, but the potions were preventative measures and wouldn't treat the actual plague. With a level difference like this one, it was doubtful whether they'd be hit with such an attack at all, but even then, it didn't hurt to be careful.

"This room looks like it might be sorta safe. Whaddaya say, Shiro?"

"Mm... Sure. Let's rest for a bit. You stay near the door, Naotsugu. I'll check in with Mari for the day. Akatsuki..."

"I'll go scout."

Without waiting for Shiroe's answer, Akatsuki melted into the darkness.

This sort of role division was already routine for the three of them. At first, Shiroe and Naotsugu hadn't been happy with the idea of sending a young girl out scouting all alone. However, Akatsuki was more than capable, and she was proud: She wanted to contribute to the party. Once they understood that (although they still hadn't approved wholeheartedly), they were able to accept this division of labor.

True, scouting was one of Akatsuki's fortes, and she was definitely the right player for the job. She was a very serious girl, and she was resolutely faithful to her mission.

Naotsugu dragged a steel box that was just the right size out of the rubble, sat down on it near the door, and began to listen, his sword out and ready. If any ratmen or other monsters approached, he'd be able to take them on instantly.

After making sure Naotsugu was settled, Shiroe half closed his eyes and opened his mental menu. He called up the telechat function and contacted Marielle. Over the four days of their journey, Shiroe had contacted her regularly, once a day. Marielle seemed to understand what he was doing, and her response came quickly.

"Thanks for all your hard work, kiddo... How's things?"

"No problems here. After I checked in yesterday, we set up camp, and early this morning, we entered the Depths of Palm."

"So you're down in a dungeon now?"

"That's right."

"How are you makin' such great time?! You're scarin' me over here! Talk about fast!"

"Mm-hm."

Marielle's warm words made him feel awkward. He wished he could think of some better way to respond, but he couldn't seem to find one. Even as he thought that, he answered conscientiously.

Marielle didn't know they were traveling by griffin. In this world, if one wanted to travel, they usually used a whistle to summon a horse. There were War Boars that were trained for use as extremely expensive items, and he'd heard that dire wolves were used in certain areas of the Chinese server. Summoners were able to summon several varieties of animal, including the unicorns they used for personal transportation. However, only a very high-level Summoner could summon animals that could carry them through the air, and no regular player would ever guess that a mere Enchanter, Warrior, and Weapon Attack player had them.

"I mean it. If we'd gone, I doubt we'd have covered half of half that distance yet. Seriously, thank you."

"Please don't worry about it… Um. How do things look?"

"I'm still gettin' through to her."

This was one of the reasons for Shiroe's daily calls. He and the others were headed to the town of Susukino in the Ezzo Empire to rescue a girl named Serara. However, they weren't able to contact Serara by telechat. The telechat function could only be used with people registered to players' friend lists, and in order to register someone to your friend list, you had to be standing right in front of them, looking at them. Since Serara wasn't on any of their lists, they couldn't contact her directly.

"So nothing's changed?"

"Nope. It sounds like she's hidin' with the nice player she mentioned. Nothing bad is happenin' right now, and she says she's all right."

"Understood. If there's someone like that in Susukino, I guess the place isn't entirely rotten."

"You said it."

Serara had been targeted by a group of vicious players who were trying to intimidate her into joining them. She'd been locked up once and had very nearly been sexually assaulted. However, she'd managed to escape, and at present, she was hiding somewhere in Susukino.

Although Susukino was the same size in area as Akiba, only about two thousand players were currently using it as their hometown, which meant its population was one-eighth the size of Akiba's. That meant that each individual player was more visible, relatively speaking. For example, if Serara went to the market to buy food, it would be several times harder for her to blend into the crowd and make her purchases quietly. With the town's population as small as it was now, Shiroe had worried that it would be nearly impossible for her to stay hidden.

However, Serara seemed to have found an ally. Shiroe didn't know the details, but the ally was a player with good intentions, and their help had made it possible for Serara to make her initial escape from the dangerous Briganteers guild.

If Serara had an ally whose identity wasn't known to the enemy, shopping would be incredibly easy. In that case, there was a good possibility that Serara could stay hidden until they got there. If there were only two thousand players in Susukino, there would be scores of deserted houses and empty buildings. The lack of players—a factor that had worked against Serara before—would now work in her favor, Shiroe thought. He felt a bit relieved.

"Since we're in a dungeon, I'm not sure what things are going to be like for a while, so I'll contact you again once we're out. I'd assumed the Tearstone Mountains would be the place that gave us the most trouble—"

"What are you goin' to do about the strait?"

"We'll think about that when we get there."

They were actually planning to fly across on the griffins, but Shiroe kept his answer vague. Although Akatsuki had accepted it as a matter of course, knowing they had mounts that could fly would earn them nothing but envy from the average player. In addition, for players that knew how they were acquired, the griffins would be proof that their owners had been victorious in the Hades's Breath full raid. Large-scale battles were high-end *Elder Tales* content. They were hard battles that only a few of the bigger guilds could attempt and average players could only dream about, and the rewards included rare items such as griffins' pipes. A certain subset of players would find it unforgivable that someone like Shiroe, a player who wasn't even in a guild, had such a rare item.

Marielle was the Crescent Moon League guild master. Unlike Shiroe, she had a large circle of acquaintances, and at the very least, it was likely that all the members of her guild knew that Shiroe, Naotsugu, and Akatsuki were on their way to Susukino to rescue one of the guild's members. Marielle would probably register the griffins with no more than her usual smile, but it wasn't a sure bet that all the members would follow suit. If word got around, people might start to look at them differently, and that idea scared Shiroe a bit.

"Well, it's you guys. I think you're gonna be just fine."

Marielle giggled at Shiroe's haphazard remark.

I know she's pushing herself to sound normal, and she still sounds like this... Mari's really strong.

"We haven't taken any major damage yet. We haven't done very much fighting at all."

"Roger that!"

"All right. I'll call again later."

"Yep! I'll be sendin' prayers to the god Eulara for you. Say hi to Naotsugu and Akatsuki for me. Henrietta's gettin' lonesome over here!"

As Marielle ended the telechat, Shiroe thought that her closing comment about the god Eulara made her really sound like a Cleric.

So far, everything's going according to plan...

"How does the situation look, my liege?"

"~~~!"

Since he'd been concentrating on the telechat, he'd completely failed to notice, but Akatsuki was back. When Shiroe turned around, Naotsugu was chowing down on some travel rations.

"No changes in Akiba. Serara is currently in hiding in Susukino, and there's no trouble on her end. The situation's stable."

"Understood."

Akatsuki answered briefly, then took a big canteen out of her pack. The canteen was actually the same size as Shiroe's, but when Akatsuki held it, it looked bigger. Shiroe handed her an orange he'd taken from his pack. Fruit could be eaten without being prepared, and in this world, where most food items tasted the same, it was the one precious thing that actually tasted like itself.

Shiroe's pack was magic and could hold up to two hundred kilograms' worth of items. The bag canceled out the weight of anything put into it, so that however much it was holding at the time, it only weighed as much as a small, empty knapsack.

This sort of magic bag was a typical *Elder Tales* magic item. There were several grades ranked by their weight limit and the types of items that could be carried, and since the bags were so convenient, almost all players had one. The packs were one of this world's must-have survival items: Thanks to them, players could keep fighting even if they found treasure in a dungeon, and they made it easy to carry food and camping gear around.

"Could you report on your scouting expedition now? I'd like to check the terrain against the map."

"Of course."

As she dexterously peeled the orange with her knife, Akatsuki reported the results of her expedition. The main road through the tunnel was so wide that even dump trucks would have no problem entering it side by side, and there was really no way to get lost on it, but that road was crossed by countless side roads. If they went straight down the main road, it would get them to their destination; however, since there were colonies of ratmen in places, they might have to make the occasional detour, and the information from Akatsuki's scouting excursions was invaluable. As he listened to her report, Shiroe jotted down new branch roads on the sheaf of paper he kept nearby.

"…Like this?"

"Yes, that looks right… You're good at this sort of thing, my liege."

Akatsuki sounded impressed. She was standing on tiptoe to look at the drawing by Shiroe's hand, inspecting the parts he'd just added.

"It's a little like CAD… That and I'm a Scribe."

"What's CAD?"

"Computer-aided drafting. I do some of it at university. On top of that, I'm in the Department of Engineering, so…"

"You're in college, my liege?"

Shiroe nodded. "I'll be graduating soon, though." Real-world matters seemed distant and increasingly unreal.

"I see. We're about the same age, then."

"Huh?"

"What, for *real*?!"

Shiroe and Naotsugu reacted to Akatsuki's comment at the exact same time.

"Is it that unexpected?"

Akatsuki responded calmly. Shiroe thought, a bit guiltily, that it was. He'd assumed Akatsuki was at least three or four years younger than he was.

"You've gotta be kidding, short stuff. You're nowhere near tall enough to be an ad— Dwah!"

A sharp, flying knee kick, launched as if to strike the words down, hit Naotsugu square in the face.

"My liege. May I kick Naotsugu the Idiot?"

"I keep *telling* you, ask *first*!"

Internally, as he listened absentmindedly to their comedy routine, Shiroe felt himself break out in a cold sweat. He hadn't actually said it, but now that he thought about it, the only reason he'd had to assume Akatsuki was younger was her height.

"And anyway, stupid Naotsugu, you harp on my height too much."

"Well, your chest is even more of a washout— Nyargh!"

That time, Naotsugu took a beautiful flying knee kick from the left. From the difference in their heights, Akatsuki had to have jumped nearly two meters straight up, but she twisted back with brilliant, nearly feline aerial form and landed lightly.

"—Akatsuki? Naotsugu's going to die."

"If you insist, my liege…"

Reluctantly, Akatsuki put some distance between herself and Naotsugu. Shiroe had privately thought she was younger as well, and even though he'd been quiet about it, he felt compelled to help Naotsugu out.

"Don't tell me… Did you think I was a minor, too, my liege?"

Unable to take Akatsuki's forceful gaze, Shiroe made a muttered confession.

"It wasn't really your height or anything— I mean, age isn't— Please don't ask."

Shiroe had thought Akatsuki was younger, but he'd never treated her as a kid. This was a world where you had to fight to survive. The sort of world where they had to battle ratmen in cavernous tunnels. Age had nothing to do with it: Anyone who couldn't do the bare minimum of what had to be done for themselves would have a hard time surviving… Even if "death" didn't technically exist.

Shiroe remembered the twins he'd helped out. Come to think of it, on the day of the Catastrophe, he'd been playing with them right up until it happened. They'd been separated when the Catastrophe kicked him back to Akiba. He'd seen them later from a distance, and they seemed to have joined a guild, but he was still a bit worried.

Once they got back to Akiba, he decided, he'd check up on them.

"My liege? What are you brooding about?"

"Hm? I'm not really thinking about anything."

"That's not true. When you think, your forehead wrinkles up right between your eyebrows."

"…Oh. Uh…"

He'd tried arguing for no real reason, but Akatsuki had seen right through him. That part wasn't so bad, but Akatsuki had begun tapping the space between her own eyebrows, saying, "Right here. Old guy wrinkles," and it was making him feel very weird.

"Rrgh! Naotsugu, what's so funny?!"

"You've gotta ask? Gwah-hah! Ha-ha-ha-ha-ha!"

Shiroe aimed a kick at Naotsugu's shin, but Naotsugu's legs were covered in thick armor, too, and he only hurt his toes.

After the three of them bickered for a while, they stood and got ready to press forward. The fathomless darkness of the tunnel pressed down on them, as heavy as eternity. The atmosphere was damp and frigid in the way peculiar to deep underground spaces, but even so, as they laughed together, the air around them felt just a little warmer.

▶ 5

By the time they finally left the endless tunnel, the first light of dawn was beginning to edge the mountains on the horizon with purple. They'd been underground for a very long time, and they stretched hugely in the cold, fresh wind. Although the cavern hadn't been so low they'd had to stoop, having several hundred million tons of earth and sand above them had been more oppressive than they'd realized. Now they were just happy to have the early summer sky, still indigo with receding night, over their heads.

"The wind is cold."

Akatsuki leapt nimbly up onto a large boulder that looked out over the forest and the ocean.

"Yeah. Feels good, though. We're finally out. Glad-that's-over city!"

Shiroe hurried after the two of them and climbed up onto the boulder. The wind was really cold, but the view was overwhelming. The primeval forest, a green so deep that it looked nearly black, was being colored with great strokes of rose-colored light. When the clouds that rode the dawn wind broke, that rosy light struck the sea that gleamed on the far horizon, making it shine raspberry and gold.

"How pretty."

"Whooooa…"

Akatsuki and Naotsugu's brief comments said it all.

Come to think of it, this is a first, Shiroe thought.

We're the first people to ever see this view… No one in this world has traveled all the way from Akiba to Susukino yet. We're really the first ones to see this. There are lots of players who happened to be passing through here at dawn when Elder Tales *was just a game, but in this other world, we're the first. And being first is…*

"—Adventures are all about firsts, you know. It's feeling like a psyched-up hamster, going *eek-brr-whizzz*, like that… Huh? What was that? 'Don't wet your pants?' Hey, why not, it's fun! …It's not fun? It is too! I mean, look at this fantabulous thing we got to see! Talk about making out like bandits! Ha-ha-ha-ha-ha!!"

She'd said that. She'd been randomly brimming over with confidence, filled with conviction even though she had zero proof, a girl made up entirely of whims and exaggerations and energy… And even then, she'd always known the right answer. If she'd been here, she'd have worn this view with pride, like a medal of honor.

That was why Shiroe spoke to the other two, saying exactly what he felt.

"We're the first. We're the very first Adventurers in this other world to see this view."

It was the first time Shiroe had consciously declared that this was another world.

The breathtaking natural beauty that spread out below them said it more plainly than any logical quibble ever could. No game could hold a view like this. The dawn wind, the cool air, the faint noises that came to them across the treetops, the early morning scenery that changed by the millisecond—none of it would be possible for a jumped-up VR environment.

When he'd come to this world, and when everyone around him was panicking, and when some of the players had lost their purpose in life and public order had begun to deteriorate, a part of Shiroe had stayed calm. True, he'd thought, *Not good, not good. This is a definite problem*, but he'd still gone into town every day, explored the zones, tried out spells as he battled, and meticulously determined what he could and could not do here.

…It could be that I'm better at adapting than I thought. It could be because Naotsugu was here, joking around and making me forget about the pain. It could be because we met up with Akatsuki, and things got livelier, and it helped.

Those elements had definitely been there, but now Shiroe understood that they hadn't been the whole reason. The beauty he'd felt in Akiba's ruins, buried by ancient trees, when he'd first come to this world. As if he'd felt another world there.

This is another world, and I am an Adventurer.

For a moment, Akatsuki gazed at him with a puzzled expression. Then she nodded firmly, as if she'd satisfied herself of something. Naotsugu gave a mischievous, macho smile and drew in a lungful of air.

"Right. We got here first. I've never seen a view this awesome, even in *Elder Tales*."

"It's our first trophy."

The two of them looked at the scenery as if it were something to be treasured. Then they nodded to Shiroe.

As if in response, Shiroe took out his griffin's pipe and sent a loud note toward the eastern sky.

CHAPTER.

5

ESCAPE

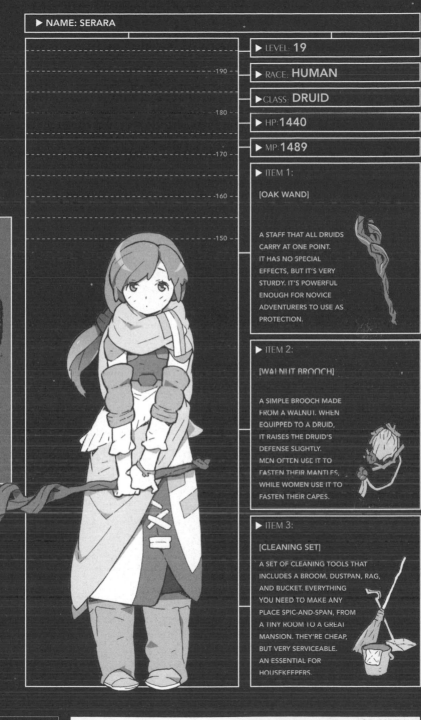

▶ LEVEL: **19**

▶ RACE: **HUMAN**

▶ CLASS: **DRUID**

▶ HP: **1440**

▶ MP: **1489**

▶ ITEM 1:

[OAK WAND]

A STAFF THAT ALL DRUIDS CARRY AT ONE POINT. IT HAS NO SPECIAL EFFECTS, BUT IT'S VERY STURDY. IT'S POWERFUL ENOUGH FOR NOVICE ADVENTURERS TO USE AS PROTECTION.

▶ ITEM 2:

[WALNUT BROOCH]

A SIMPLE BROOCH MADE FROM A WALNUT. WHEN EQUIPPED TO A DRUID, IT RAISES THE DRUID'S DEFENSE SLIGHTLY. MEN OFTEN USE IT TO FASTEN THEIR MANTLES, WHILE WOMEN USE IT TO FASTEN THEIR CAPES.

▶ ITEM 3:

[CLEANING SET]

A SET OF CLEANING TOOLS THAT INCLUDES A BROOM, DUSTPAN, RAG, AND BUCKET. EVERYTHING YOU NEED TO MAKE ANY PLACE SPIC-AND-SPAN, FROM A TINY ROOM TO A GREAT MANSION. THEY'RE CHEAP, BUT VERY SERVICEABLE. AN ESSENTIAL FOR HOUSEKEEPERS.

<Glasses>
Vision correction devices. They'll
make you very popular with a
certain type of person.

► **1**

Serara was hiding in one of the many simple insulated houses in Susukino. About the size of a normal two-bedroom apartment, it had been built inside an abandoned building. The enormous structures that were scattered across this world were remnants of the culture of the old era, which had been lost when the world collapsed. Of course, as a player, Serara knew the world design had been based on contemporary Japan. Susukino's model was the Sapporo neighborhood of the same name, and the player town held traces of the real city.

In the real world, Susukino was a red-light district, and the city held lots of mixed-use buildings. In *Elder Tales*, the city's design had been modified to consist mostly of fortresslike buildings reinforced with rough blue steel. The design motif for Hokkaido—or, in *Elder Tales* terms, the Ezzo Empire—had a boxy, retro machine empire feel to it. Its buildings, their steel frames reinforced with screws and enormous nuts and bolts, stood up well to the wind and snow, but they did nothing to keep out the bitter cold of winter. To cope, the people of Susukino had taken to building new houses of insulated materials inside the fortresslike mixed-use buildings. These smaller houses were created with an emphasis on warmth and livability. In terms of area per resident, it was terribly inefficient, and it wouldn't have been practical in the real-world Japan, but it was perfectly possible in the *Elder Tales* game world.

Serara had been using one of these insulated houses as a hideaway (her roommate, the person who had rescued her, had rented it for the two of them), and all day long, she cleaned the house's two connecting common rooms.

It wasn't that she particularly liked cleaning, and the house certainly wasn't that cluttered or dirty. There just wasn't anything else to do. TV and the Internet didn't exist in this world, which meant that killing time was no easy task. Besides, Serara was a Housekeeper. That particular subclass granted players special skills for cleaning zones, taking care of small articles, and maintaining all sorts of supplies and furnishings.

…Why on earth did I choose such a minor, useless subclass?

Serara sighed—she'd sighed so often that by now she'd completely lost track of how often—and even then, she kept right on cleaning.

In *Elder Tales*, main classes were selected when players created their characters, and they couldn't be changed later. However, if a player could stand to see their subclass experience points reset to zero, they could change subclasses with relative ease.

Serara's main class was Druid, one of the recovery classes. Serara had started playing this game, which other people said was deep and complex, because she'd thought it would be fun to play merchant.

There were lots of players who played this way. There was a unique pleasure in interacting with other players and saving up money, and it was just one of the many play styles in *Elder Tales*.

Of course, players who were playing as merchants generally chose the Merchant or Accountant subclasses, since these subclasses granted bonuses with regard to business deals and let players get slight discounts when trading with non-player characters. A production-related subclass would have been another sound option. Playing as a merchant while making a variety of items was one of the major ways to play *Elder Tales*. However, Serara had checked an introductory site when she started playing the game, and it had told her that in order to become a Merchant or an Accountant, one's ability score needed to be above a certain level and a quest had to be completed. It also said that it was hard to advance in the production subclasses if a player didn't have at least a little capital to use to buy materials.

In that case, the best plan was for her to save up some money while she leveled up in her main class, Druid, then switch to another subclass once she'd gained a bit of leeway. Whether she ended up buying in wares or just making purchases somewhere, she'd have assets and her main class level, and it wasn't as though they'd get in the way... And so she'd picked the easiest-looking subclass, just to fill in the category, and that subclass had been Housekeeper.

In other words, Serara had become a Housekeeper nearly by chance, simply because it was the only option that hadn't been eliminated.

Arrrrgh... If I'd known this was going to happen, I would have picked a production subclass even if I couldn't level up for a while. Artificer would have been nice, or Tailor...

As her thoughts ran in circles, Serara wiped down the table with a dry cloth.

The interior of the simple house looked rustic. More accurately, it *was* rustic: It was built of wood, beautiful wood grain patterns were visible in the floorboards, there was a wooden inset ceiling, and the walls looked like they belonged to a log cabin. The Ezzo Empire was a treasure trove of natural resources, and it was known as one of the most prominent mining and forestry areas on the Japanese server. Both the floorboards and the deep amber table were practically Ezzo Empire specialty products, and a careful polishing was all it took to give them a lustrous shine.

Serara, a plain girl in a loose flannel shirt and jeans with her hair pulled back in a ponytail, worked her way carefully around the log house. She wore no makeup, and although she wasn't a rare beauty, she had a fresh, neat air about her. She could easily have been mistaken for a young wife.

I'm so bored that I keep accidentally leveling up, too...

Serara sighed and opened her menu. She'd gotten more Housekeeper experience points today. Subclass levels and experience points were completely independent from the main class, and the system was very simple: Every time you accumulated ten experience points, you leveled up. The level maximum was probably 90 or 100. She'd been leveling up at an astounding pace lately, gaining three levels nearly every day. Yesterday, her Housekeeper level had been 42, and today it was already 44. If she kept this up, she'd complete the Housekeeper subclass while she was lying low in Susukino.

*Please don't let me max out my skills while I'm living like a hermit...
That would just be sad.*

Anybody who cleaned and did laundry and chores all day, every day, was bound to level up. Even Serara thought this was really more like being a housewife than a housekeeper. To a girl of her age, the word had quite a pleasant ring to it, but the embarrassment was stronger.

Look at you, you lucky thing! A young lady tidying the house for her new cat husband... Kidding! I'm kidding!

Having managed to embarrass herself, Serara began busily polishing dishes. As far as ways to kill time went, it wasn't the sort of thing that would disturb other people, and a casual observer would have called the scene peaceful.

"Serara, are mew there? I'm home."

The door opened—the house was an independent zone, which they were renting by the month, so only registered players could enter—and a very odd man came in. He was a Felinoid. Felinoids were demihumans with catlike characteristics, and one of the eight playable races in *Elder Tales*. His slender build and green corduroy jacket made him look like a medieval musketeer from a children's picture book. His long, thin arms and legs made him seem incredibly slim. His round head topped by two triangular ears could easily have been the head of a mischievous cat from a fairy tale, and the whiskers that stuck out on either side were simultaneously gallant and cute.

His name was Nyanta.

"Welcome back, Nyanta."

Serara ducked her head in a little bow.

"How was the town?"

Nyanta tilted his head a bit to one side and gave an ambiguous smile. His eyes were always slightly narrowed, as if he were smiling; it gave him a reassuring air, but it made it hard for Serara to read the nuances of his expression.

"The same as mewsual. Not too good, not too bad."

At his words, Serara's face clouded. Nyanta might have said "not too bad," but if things hadn't gotten better, it meant they were still pretty bad.

Public order in Susukino was steadily deteriorating. Since the population was small, its self-purification function wasn't functioning. Right now, the only law in Susukino was the law of the jungle. A large part of the problem was one guild known as the Briganteers. The guild was made up of notorious players who'd been run out of Akiba and Minami, and even when *Elder Tales* was a game, it hadn't had a good reputation. The Briganteers had always put profit above everything else and run roughshod over other players, and when the Catastrophe hit, they'd become something next door to a real gang of bandits practically overnight. Player kills were an everyday thing for them. Sometimes they weren't satisfied with the items they got from player killing—only half of whatever the player had been carrying— and used intimidation or persistent harassment to extort money and goods from other players. Their abuse even extended to non-player characters.

As a general rule, there was no reason for non-player characters to be targeted for ill treatment. For example, the guards who protected noncombat zones had high levels and strong combat abilities, so they could easily beat back any attack from a normal player. The non-player characters in field zones—such as traveling merchants, farm folk, and town residents who gave hints about quests—had very low combat abilities and were unable to defend themselves, but they didn't have the sort of property a player would have. On top of that, since some non-player characters did provide hints about quests, most players would never consider attacking them.

However, the Briganteers didn't care. Not only that, but they'd begun to do something that rendered even the non-player characters' lack of property meaningless: They'd turned the non-player characters themselves into property. In other words, they'd become slave traders.

In *Elder Tales*, as in other games, it was possible for players to employ non-player characters. There were all sorts of reasons for doing this, but the most common one was to hire someone to take care of your house. In *Elder Tales*, where players could buy houses, there was steady demand for people to clean and manage personal residences. Whether you were buying or renting, if you didn't regularly clean the zone where you lived, the maintenance fees went up. Non-player characters with certain types of special abilities could be very useful in guild activities, although they couldn't be taken into battle. It wasn't at all unusual to employ non-player characters this way.

One of the reasons Serara's Housekeeper subclass was such a minor one was that non-player characters could do the job just as well. If you employed a Maid non-player character, for example, for about eight hundred gold coins a month, any dwelling up to the size of a small manor would be kept neat and tidy at all times. No wonder fewer players were seeking to level up their Housekeeper skills.

Of course, even if it was exquisitely designed, *Elder Tales* was only an online RPG. Maids, Harvesters, Assistants, and a few other exceptional non-player characters would use their special abilities to help players, but they were the minority. Ordinary non-player characters couldn't be hired. Although their models were the same as the ones used for player characters, their communication abilities were limited to elementary AI, and they couldn't do anything except give preset keyword information or fill in their side of a multiple-choice-directed conversation. In other words, they shouldn't have been worth attacking.

However, the Catastrophe had destroyed several things that had once been common knowledge. The game had turned real, and daily routine had become a nightmare. Since the Catastrophe, it would have been just as easy to count the stars as it would have been to count the major changes that had occurred, but the changes in the non-player characters had been particularly mind-boggling. In this world, they were real, flesh-and-blood beings, and they could move and converse almost as well as regular players. Of course, unless their settings specified otherwise, their combat abilities and specialized skills were far inferior to players' skills, but these days it was often hard to tell whether you were talking to a player or a non-player character without checking the menu screen.

Another important point was that the non-player character population had exploded.

The non-player characters were incredibly close to human, and there were a lot more of them. When these two facts had been dangled in front of the crafty Briganteers like ripe fruit, the result had been the invention of "slave trading for fun."

Of course, since Susukino's population was just two thousand, there wasn't a huge market. It was an ugly caricature of economic activity, not something done for profit.

Appallingly, even hunting non-player characters had become a way to kill time. And, as with all stupidity, it had escalated, and the abuse and extortion that had been focused on non-player characters had been turned on Serara, a real female player.

As she remembered, Serara felt the blood drain from her face. A dark veil seemed to fall across her vision, and she could feel her temperature dropping. If Nyanta hadn't saved her, she knew something terrible would have happened.

"Come now, Serara, it's all right. Don't brood like that. If you think too hard, mew'll be old before mew know it."

Nyanta waved a hand in front of Serara's eyes.

"At times like this, it's better to eat some fruit and not think very hard at all... Here."

As Serara nodded very slightly, he handed her an apple. It was bright red, and its sweet, carrying fragrance was somehow reassuring.

"The house is mewtiful again today. Mew'll make some lucky fellow a fine wife someday, Serara."

Nyanta spoke in a leisurely voice, pulling a chair out from the kitchen table and sitting down.

At his words, Serara felt her chilled body grow warm again.

"Oh no, that's not true. Not at all."

Nyanta referred to himself as an old man. From his voice, he was certainly much older than Serara. She was a high school junior, and she thought he could easily be more than twice her age. No matter what he said, though, he didn't seem at all elderly. When she'd told him so once, he'd said, "That's just the game graphics," but Serara didn't think so at all.

Nyanta must be a...a dashing middle-aged man. I'm sure of it. He's stylish and handsome and mature and eloquent...

Yes, it was a game, and yes, the graphics were designed to be beautiful, but as far as Serara was concerned, once you started playing alongside someone, appearance didn't matter at all. In the post-Catastrophe world, that went double. Since she'd been living with Nyanta (even though it was only because it was an emergency), she'd gotten to know him very well.

Nyanta seemed like a reliable, mature man. Although there was nothing rough about him at all, being around him was oddly reassuring, as if she knew she'd be protected. His bushy, marvelous silver ears could have belonged to a purebred cat, and his slim build was quite smart.

The only trouble is, since Nyanta's so stylish, I look chunky when we're together... I am a bit pudgy, I guess...

Most people would have said that Serara simply had a womanly figure, but Nyanta seemed to give her a bit of a complex. On the other hand, although Nyanta did have a considerable amount of muscle on him, at first glance he seemed to have been put together from pencils.

"Any mews from the rescue party?"

Nyanta asked this as he unpacked his shopping bag at the table. Both Serara and Nyanta knew that the Crescent Moon League, Serara's guild, was sending a rescue squad of three players from Akiba to Susukino, and it had been a common topic of discussion lately. The squad was traveling so rapidly that even Nyanta was impressed. Although Serara couldn't contact them directly, Marielle, the Crescent Moon League guild master, called her several times a day with updates, so Serara knew roughly where they were.

"Yes, they're almost here. She said they should arrive sometime before noon tomorrow," Serara reported.

Once the rescue party arrived, she'd go back to Akiba with them. She couldn't stay in a place like Susukino forever.

...But what would Nyanta do? Serara still wasn't able to ask him. Nyanta had saved her because he was a good man, not because he wanted anything, and Serara didn't know how much she could hope for from him. She felt as if she'd already received far more than she could repay, but every time she brought it up, he just smiled and dodged the question, saying, "It is the duty—and the pleasure—of the elderly to help young people."

It's very nice of him to say so, but... It does mean he's treating me like a kid...

"Just a little more patience, then. I'm sure it's been rough on mew, being cooped up in this tiny house, but it won't be much longer now. Don't worry. They'll get mew out and home safely."

At Nyanta's smile, Serara lost yet another chance to ask him.

▶ 2

Another afternoon and night had passed. As scheduled, Shiroe, Naotsugu, and Akatsuki had set up camp for reconnaissance about fifteen minutes from the outskirts of Susukino. The town of Susukino, the imperial capital of Ezzo, was an urban zone located in the Ezzo Empire field zone, roughly where Sapporo had been in the old world. The area was a fortified city that included a farming region where many non-player characters lived.

When Shiroe, cautious as usual, found a tumbledown house on the outskirts of the city where they wouldn't be spotted, they settled there for a while and checked the gates to the Susukino zone.

"I see nothing that currently warrants caution, my liege."

"The place sure feels dicey, though. It's practically dead."

Shiroe nodded agreement with both these statements. He was drawing a simple map of Susukino on a piece of paper he'd taken from an inner pocket.

"Susukino is built around a main street... Like so. The downtown area cuts across the east side. The central plaza is here in the east. We"—he drew in an arrow—"are going to enter from the west."

"Couldn't we just rendezvous with them outside the city?"

"Bad plan, short stuff."

"Is it, Naotsugu the Lech?"

Shutting down his companions, who'd started their usual short-stuff-and-lech banter, Shiroe explained.

"Akiba was the last city we visited. That means if we get wiped out, our corpses will get taken back to Akiba after a little while and revived there... But we're here to rescue Serara, and she's different. If she dies, she'll revive in Susukino. In other words, even if the rendezvous goes without a hitch, if something happens and we all die, we'll end up in Akiba, Serara will end up in Susukino, and we'll have to start all over again. I want to avoid that."

"I see. You're right."

Akatsuki conceded gracefully. Naotsugu wore a satisfied expression that seemed to say, "What did I tell you?"

"Next, I want to confirm our formation. Akatsuki... I want you using Sneak and Silent Move right from the beginning. Follow us, but make sure no one can tell you're there, plea—"

"Quit being polite."

"Agh... Right. Okay. Naotsugu, you and I will walk in through the gate normally. You come in with us, Akatsuki, but make sure you're not detected. We'll head for the abandoned building we're using as a rendezvous point. Akatsuki, you find a place to hide somewhere in the area and keep an eye on the whole building. If there's any trouble, alert me by telechat."

The black-haired girl nodded, her face sober.

"Naotsugu, you take up a position near the building's entrance. If possible, find a place where you can see both the street and the inside of the building. Wait there and be ready to respond to trouble, inside or out. I'll go on into the building and meet up with Serara, and the two of us will come back to where you are as quickly as possible."

"Roger that. So, uh, what about the third party that's been helping her out?"

"I'm not sure yet. Personally, I'd like to get them out of Susukino when we go, whether or not they want to travel all the way back to Akiba with us."

Shiroe was thinking hard as he spoke.

"There's a very real possibility that the guild we're assuming is behind most of the trouble in Susukino has Serara registered as a friend."

Unlike the mutual consent the function's name implied, as long as a player was in front of a person, one could register them as a friend without their permission. Once they were on a friend list, a person would be able to tell whether the other player was online or not and even whether the two of them were in the same zone.

"If they have, there's a good chance they'll know she's in Susukino the second she leaves the room where she's been hiding. They may send people after her. It would be better to get away from Susukino before that happens. If we put two or three zones between us and the city, they won't follow us… At least, I don't think they will."

Serara was currently in a safe house somewhere in Susukino, and they'd been told that the house was an independent zone inside an abandoned building. In other words, as long as she was hiding in that smaller zone, even if Serara had been friended by the troublemakers, they wouldn't be able to tell she was still in their zone. That said, once she left that safe house and entered the larger Susukino zone, it was best to assume that the Briganteers would know. On top of that, there was no way for her to return to Akiba without passing through Susukino.

This strategy was one Shiroe had come up with on the journey to Susukino in order to get around the issue, and he was able to explain it smoothly. He'd put together the fairly elaborate formation just to be safe; he thought the possibility of real trouble was quite low. However, it depended on how tenacious and unscrupulous the Susukino problem guild was. This wouldn't be like hunting monsters: If their group got wiped out, they wouldn't just be able to go back to the town and start over.

—Worst-case scenarios happen all the time. I know it's thoughts like this that make people say I'm too introverted and overthinking things, but still…

If he was worrying over nothing, so be it. He really hoped he was. Naotsugu and Akatsuki nodded in emphatic agreement.

"So we could be kissing Susukino good-bye in an hour or so."

"I'll support your strategy, my liege."

After going over several detailed call signs and deciding how to meet back up in an emergency, the three of them departed for Susukino.

The gate of the city was overwhelming. Reinforced with blue steel, it had been designed to look like a castle gate, and it had angular latches jutting into the frame on all sides. The Ezzo Empire was a young nation founded by the conquering emperor Al Rahdil. Its background information said it was a bellicose country with a strong military. That meant that weapons were carried prominently around town, and banners of all colors lent the country a wartime atmosphere.

It really doesn't feel like Akiba. I was here when Elder Tales *was a game, but the atmosphere now is in a whole different league...*

All the things Shiroe had ignored as unimportant background when this was a game—like the town's decorations, its smell, and all the other details—struck him as fresh and novel now. Naotsugu, wrapped in a thick wool mantle, seemed to feel the same way; he was looking around curiously.

A long main street stretched toward the urban area. It was crowded with non-player characters, but their faces all seemed listless and drained. The players they saw also looked dispirited, and many of them wore very troubled expressions.

"The atmosphere really tanks. I wouldn't want to live here."

Naotsugu kept his voice low so he wouldn't be overheard.

"Agreed," Shiroe murmured.

Although he did sympathize with the people here, a much larger part of him was supremely irritated. He'd felt the irritation during their journey as well, but on reaching the city, it had abruptly grown too big to control. He was annoyed. He was angry. The unpleasant feelings seemed to be ratcheting his temperature up. Still, although he wanted to do *something* to improve matters, at this point, he didn't have either the power or the means.

Shiroe looked back warily several times, but he couldn't sense Akatsuki there at all, and he had no idea where she was. He thought she was probably following them, but she'd managed to erase her presence so completely that it made him uneasy.

After a short while, an abandoned building with a broken sign that read RAOKE BO clinging to it came into view. That was the landmark they'd been told about in their meeting with Marielle. Shiroe gave a small wave, signaling, and he and Naotsugu entered the building.

The cracked concrete had been reinforced with steel here and there, and it was in better shape than similar buildings in Akiba. It looked as though the concrete was still sturdy, at any rate. As soon as Naotsugu stepped into the building, he turned right, checking the guardroom. Shiroe could hear faint sounds from deeper inside. Letting a small part

of his mind keep track of them, he headed farther into the building and climbed the stairs to the second floor.

When he contacted Marielle via telechat and had her relay the information, the response that came back was "We'll head over right away." Up to this point, everything had gone according to plan, and Shiroe let himself relax just a little. It had been six minutes since they'd entered Susukino. So far, so good.

"Um, hello?"

Shiroe, who'd turned calmly enough at the sound of approaching footsteps, was greeted by a girl wearing the softly curving leather armor unique to the recovery classes. Her hair hung down her back in a ponytail, and the eyes that gazed up at him seemed a bit apologetic. When combined with her shy, nervous attitude, it made Shiroe think of a small animal who'd poked its face out of the woods. He gave her a slight smile.

"I'm Serara of the Crescent Moon guild. Thank you so much for doing this." The girl gave a light bow, but—

"Mrowr."

"—Captain?! Wha… It's *you*!"

Shiroe yelled at the top of his lungs, accidentally—and rudely—ignoring Serara.

"Well, well! If it isn't Shiroechi. I did think this was an unmewsually fast and daring rescue."

The tall shadow that stood there, guarding Serara's back, was the Debauchery Tea Party's own captain and feline retiree, the cat-eared Swashbuckler Nyanta.

▶ 3

Even for a Debauchery Tea Party member, Nyanta had been a player with a unique style. He was mild mannered, and he always had a tranquil, unconcerned air about him that made him seem a little like a sunbathing cat. He'd brought an invaluable element of common sense to the Debauchery Tea Party, which had many members who loved excitement and were prone to get out of control.

Nyanta said he was "an old man," and coming from him, the words had the genuine ring of mature calm to them. The voice chat function in *Elder Tales* meant it was perfectly possible to deduce a player's age from their voice. Although Nyanta claimed to be old, Shiroe didn't think he'd reached fifty. He was more likely to be in his forties or possibly a sober, dignified individual in his thirties.

Of course, the average age in network games was low. Players in their thirties weren't rare, but players in their forties were few and far between. This might have been what Nyanta was thinking of when he called himself an old man, but Shiroe and the people around him thought differently. In this case, "mature adult" had nothing to do with actual age. It was Nyanta's personality and the experience evident in his words and gestures that made others acknowledge him as an adult, and when they said "adult," they didn't mean the much-loathed term used by children to designate "those clueless people who spoil all our fun." They meant something different, an adviser who was always there, looking out for them when they needed him.

Nyanta had never hesitated to lend a listening ear to a conflicted friend or a troubled group member. Although he wasn't overbearing in his help, his calm voice made players feel as though they could tackle even problems that had seemed insurmountable, and his younger companions had real respect for him. His nicknames "Captain" and "the Retiree" had been friendly gestures from the group as well.

The Debauchery Tea Party had been a simple gathering of players, not a guild. Many of its members had been unaffiliated, but of course there had been several who were members of guilds of all stripes. However, as a rule, large, well-regulated guilds didn't like their members mixing too freely with outsiders. This wasn't simply baseless prejudice (although it could occasionally be that): The guilds were worried about losing their internal human resources. For example, if a high-level player who belonged to a guild was going to be out coaching new players who weren't part of the guild and younger players who belonged to other guilds, of course his guild would want him to coach their own younger players instead. At base, guilds were mutual aid organizations used by players to compensate for their own shortcomings. From that perspective, it was only natural that most Debauchery

Tea Party members who had other affiliations belonged to small or midsized guilds.

Nyanta had belonged to the guild Cat Kibble. That said, Shiroe had never seen a Cat Kibble member besides Nyanta. Forget midsized or small, the guild had to have been practically nonexistent. When Shiroe had asked Nyanta about it, he'd laughed and said, "It feels a bit like I've found a veranda that suits me, but the house is falling to pieces."

In that case, had Nyanta been an important adviser to the Debauchery Tea Party or the power behind it? The answer was no. In fact, it seemed to Shiroe that Nyanta had been almost afraid of influencing the group's direction. He'd suspected that although Nyanta's attitude and way of enjoying the game were sedate, he'd actually liked the Debauchery Tea Party's frequent shenanigans and he'd wanted to have fun as part of the group of so-called "kids."

"Oh... I, uh, I'm sorry, Miss Serara. My name is Shiroe. I'm a friend of the Retiree here."

"That's right, Serara. This is Shiroechi, and he's a very good, clever boy. A mewly promising young fellow. If he's the one who's come for mew, this plan is bound to succeed."

"I see your forced 'mews' are alive and well, Captain."

Shiroe smiled mischievously. He'd had fun picking on Nyanta's mews since their Tea Party days.

"Why, whatever do mew mean, Shiroechi? This is mewniversal Felinoid speech. And what amewsing speech it is, if a bit rough around the edges."

"'Mew,' 'ruff'... Pick a species, Captain."

Nyanta and Shiroe's cheerful exchange seemed to have thoroughly unsettled Serara. She finally pulled herself together enough to ask, "You two know each other, then?"

"Oh, I'd say we do. I once asked Shiroechi to groom me for fleas."

"I have no memory of doing any such thing."

Further unsettled, Serara could only nod silently.

"If you're here, Shiroechi... Who are the other two?"

"One's Naotsugu. The other is a girl named Akatsuki, a level-ninety Assassin. During team training, she got one hundred and sixty units in ten days. She's really good."

"So Naotsugucchi's here, too, is he? And a mew companion? … That's fine mews. It looks like it's your time at last, Shiroechi."

Nyanta's eyes were always slightly narrowed as if he were smiling, but as he looked at Shiroe, his smile deepened slightly.

"Captain Nyanta… What happened to Cat Kibble?"

"The poor old house couldn't take the wind and snow. It collapsed. I may leave Susukino and make my way down to Akiba with mew."

Nyanta's words seemed more transparent than lonely.

"What do you…? Oh. Hang on."

Just as Shiroe was about to ask what he meant, a soft chime sounded in his ear.

"A group is approaching your building. They look rough. The leader may be a Monk. Three Weapon Attack classes, two healers. They seem to have formed a party. They're fanning out to block the street as they approach. They could be there in as little as two minutes."

At Akatsuki's concise telechat, Shiroe visualized the map he'd been drawing a short while ago, the one of Susukino's streets.

"There's a group coming this way. A party of six led by a Monk. Sound familiar?"

"That's—!"

"That's probably the Briganteers leader, Demiquas. He's a level-ninety Monk, and his friends' levels will be similar. He's the one behind this affair… The enemy."

Nyanta said "enemy" very clearly. In the game, he'd never used that word to refer to other players, but now he said it decisively and without hesitation. Hearing that settled Shiroe's resolve, too.

"Does this building have a back door? We'll force our way through if we have to."

▶4

"This way, mew two."

"Are you all right, Miss Serara?"

"O-of course."

Serara desperately followed Nyanta, who was running in the lead.

Shiroe, the young man who'd come to rescue her, was right behind her.

So he's a friend of Nyanta's... He looks a little hard to please, but he seems really smart, she thought, remembering Shiroe's sharp eyes.

She snuck a glance behind her. Shiroe was scanning the area and talking in a low voice. Probably a telechat. His training showed through in the fact that he didn't stumble.

The Briganteers seemed to have been suspicious of the simple housing district for a while, and they were searching it exhaustively. Serara thought their friend lists must have alerted them when she'd moved from the safe house into the Susukino zone. In that case, it was only a matter of time until they found them. The layout of Susukino was a simple grid, and most roads intersected with each other at right angles. Even if they ran through the backstreets, if the enemy had enough members, they'd eventually be caught.

Knowing that, Nyanta and Shiroe had chosen to force their way through instead. They said it was a gamble they'd have to take at some point if they were going to return to Akiba. Naotsugu and Akatsuki hadn't been spotted yet, and Shiroe had probably contacted them via telechat. They were currently moving toward the broad avenue to the west, hurrying but not panicking.

In the end, their guess proved to be correct: Briganteers guild members were loitering at the gate as well.

"Susukino is a noncombat zone. What mew they think they're doing...?"

"They're probably planning to let us walk for now."

Shiroe had said "for now," and it really would be only temporary. The guild would mount their real offensive once they were out of the noncombat zone. Serara thought that was the strategy the Briganteers had put together and that Shiroe and Nyanta were fully aware of it.

"Do mew think so?"

Nyanta didn't question Shiroe's abbreviated comment, possibly out of consideration for Serara. However, the calm in his voice was completely different from what it usually was. It was a difference Serara couldn't quite define, but it made her shiver involuntarily.

"What... What should I do?"

Her voice was shaking. Demiquas had grabbed her wrist once. The mere memory of his grotesquely muscle-bound arm and his ugly smile made her heart wilt.

"…Let's see."

Shiroe seemed to be gazing into the distance. She saw the expression silently drain from his profile. Abruptly, he looked far more intelligent and much, much colder, and she felt a little afraid of him.

"If they're going to let us out, let's take them up on it. If we can get outside the city, so much the better."

"…What?"

At Shiroe's words, Serara's eyes widened.

If they left the city, they'd be outside the noncombat zone. If they were captured, they'd have to fight, and the Briganteers had enough members to guard all the avenues leading out of the city.

Serara was sure that if it came down to combat, she, Nyanta, and Shiroe would all be killed easily. No matter how skilled Nyanta and Shiroe were and no matter how high level Shiroe's reinforcements were, there were only five of them altogether. Besides, that five included Serara herself, and she wasn't even level 30. If the Briganteers decided to PK them, she was sure they wouldn't have a chance. Of course they wouldn't. They were far too outnumbered.

"Even if we manage to get away without a fight, we'll need to make them slip up. If they start pursuing us when they're this close to us, even after we're away from Susukino, they'll probably follow us until doomsday. The enemy must know you have people helping you, Miss Serara. You wouldn't have been able to keep yourself fed otherwise. I assume they also know you don't have very many allies. Taken together, that means that the Briganteers plan to surround and PK us once we've gotten a little distance from the noncombat zone. They'll try to take out your allies first. Then they'll break your will and get you under their control. I think they'll have settled on that course at this point."

Shiroe's words sounded completely analytical. To Serara, he seemed detached from the situation.

"But they'll kill us! How can you just—"

"Serara, Serara, it's all right. Mew mustn't let yourself get so flustered. If Shiroechi says that's how things are, then that's how they are. And if he's here, then there's nothing to worry about."

Nyanta's words were casual and relaxed, completely divorced from Serara's anxiety and terror. Shiroe had gotten information on the Briganteers members and fighting strength from Nyanta, but as far as Serara could see, their situation was fairly dire. She didn't understand how they could be so calm.

"Captain."

"Yes?"

"If you fought their leader one-on-one…?"

Shiroe asked, and Nyanta nodded.

"Now that *is* a stupid question."

His response startled Serara. She'd heard that Nyanta was a veteran player, but fighting PKs was nothing like fighting monsters. That had been true even when *Elder Tales* was an online game. Unlike monsters, which had a limited range of attack techniques and were driven by instinct, there was no telling what players would do. The tension during combat was dozens of times greater, and even the most skillful fighter would make mistakes—or at least that was what Henrietta had told Serara. Serara had never seen a player so skilled that they could consent to a PK battle this readily.

"We'll go with that strategy, then. First, the three of us will leave the zone together. Once we've come far enough that we won't be able to run back into the town, the Briganteers will launch their PK battle. Once we take out the enemy boss, we'll use the opportunity to make our escape."

But that's ridiculous!

Serara felt herself go pale.

That wasn't a strategy. It was practically leaving everything to chance. It seemed almost like suicide. She tried to speak up, to take him to task over it, but she couldn't even find the words.

"Perfect. Mew haven't changed a bit, Shiroechi."

On top of that, incredibly, Nyanta seemed to be in total agreement with Shiroe. When Serara turned, startled, Nyanta widened his narrow right eye at her.

"I haven't ripped someone to pieces in a very long time. Make sure and watch closely, Serara. It's all right. I won't let them lay a finger on mew."

At that, Serara swore to herself that she'd brave any terror, if only Nyanta would fight to protect her.

▶ 5

…And now the situation had played out just as Shiroe and the others had anticipated. They'd passed through the gate under the crude stares of the Briganteers. As Serara and the others went through, about ten of the ruffians followed them, keeping their distance. They were probably planning to attack as soon as they were away from the town. Even Serara, who had never directly encountered bloodlust, seemed to sense that surge of emotion, something between malice and spite. Her shoulders were trembling.

I can't reasonably ask her to trust me.

Shiroe was fully aware of Serara's anxiety. To some extent, her fears were correct. The Briganteers were a force to be reckoned with. It was no wonder she doubted their chances of victory.

The tension in the air grew thicker with each step they took. The gate that led to Susukino receded behind them. Slowly but surely, the circle of Briganteers was closing in.

"This is far enough," Shiroe murmured.

Then he raised his voice.

"Excuse me! Which of you gentlemen is Demiquas of the Briganteers?"

His words caused a stir in the players that surrounded them. They hadn't expected such a clear challenge.

"No, no. Shiroechi, my boy. It's rude to bellow questions at people like that. I know who he is. He's that big fellow over there. Oooooy, Demiquas!"

The burly man who stepped from the crowd, as if drawn by Nyanta's voice, was the Briganteers leader, Demiquas. His powerfully muscled torso was sheathed in tight-fitting light armor that resembled a singlet, and he wore weapons that looked like tiger claws on both hands.

Although he'd been modeled on the same polygon data as everyone else and should have been quite handsome, his coarse expression mirrored the man inside.

"So you're the punks who've been buzzing around Serara?"

"Ah, that was just me. And 'alley cat' is more apt than 'punk' really."

Nyanta corrected him, taking things at his own speed as usual. In contrast to what he was saying, his mellow voice was calm, dignified, and mature, and it dampened his opponents' urge to fight. However, his next words were cutting.

"...Young people are always reckless and wild. It's the way of the world, and maybe permitting that young enthusiasm is a virtue in adults, but there are limits."

"What are you drooling about, furry?!"

"I'm about to tell mew. Listen very closely... Demiquas. Mew've gone too far. I know you plan to attempt a player kill here, so I'll save mew the trouble. Cutting down uppity young bucks is another adult responsibility. I'll give mew the opportunity to train against an expert. Have at me."

Those are pretty strong words for the Captain, but what these guys have done is actually criminal. I guess I can't blame him.

Even as Shiroe thought that, he was using his mental menu to check the power of the enemies around them.

"Hah! What're you running on about? Who says we have to play by your rules? I've got ten guys with me here!"

"I'm sorry to interrupt. It's all right, Demiquas. It doesn't have to be you. And actually... You, sir. The player in the gray robe. That's a secret-level item from the Salamander's Cavern, isn't it? You look stronger than this fellow. I think we'd all be more satisfied with the outcome if you fought instead of the Monk. Captain Nyanta, go ahead and fight the magic user instead."

"Are you aware that I'm 'Gray Steel' Rondarg?"

"Mew have a point... Let's make sure they know what's what."

As Serara watched in shock—this was nothing like the plan they'd discussed earlier—Shiroe switched the target from Demiquas to the magic user at his side. When even Nyanta expressed agreement with the change, a ripple of bewilderment spread through the Briganteers group. Some looked at the magic user Rondarg while others watched

Demiquas, and even Shiroe's group picked up on the slight change in temperature.

So they aren't a united front. I knew it. A guild cobbled together as quickly as theirs couldn't be. That Rondarg guy is second-in-command and Demiquas's adviser. I guess we'll see how much control you have over your guild members, Demiquas. Shiroe felt his feelings go quiet, flickering like flame far below the surface.

True, Shiroe was bad at dealing with people. It was safe to say that he hated having noisy idiots hanging around... That didn't mean he couldn't handle it.

He was a pacifist, and he didn't want to fight other players.

That didn't mean he couldn't do it.

Quite the opposite, in fact.

Under the circumstances, even Shiroe could feel it. He was fully aware of the emotion, black as the ocean at night, that was filling his heart. It was rooted in his irritation, and it was an impulse toward destruction.

Rip someone to pieces, Nyanta had said.

His usual peaceful, sunlit smile had crumbled, and his grin had revealed feline fangs. Even Shiroe had similar fangs, deep inside. Shiroe's unconscious was convinced that those who lived by the sword should be prepared to die by the sword. No mercy would be shown here.

"'Gray Steel' Rondarg, wasn't it? A byname, that's impressive. Yes, you'll suit us much better than Demiquas over there... This is Captain Nyanta, your opponent. He's a Swashbuckler. Let's begin the duel. We don't intend to run."

"Let's hurry and get started. From your equipment, mew seem to be a first-class professional. This is your way, isn't it? Mewsing combat to settle scores once and for all. Demiquas insists on a group attack because he fears my rapiers, poor soul. We'll just ignore him."

Nyanta's insult proved to be the last straw. Enraged, Demiquas stalked up to stand in front of Nyanta, his expression a mixture of anger and tension and scorn.

"Fine, joker. I'll take you on. I'll give you a one-way ticket to hell... *with my fist!*"

Under the pretense of accepting a one-on-one battle, Demiquas threw a punch at Nyanta, putting all his strength behind the surprise attack. Watching the punch as it headed straight for his nose, Nyanta evaded, leaping back several meters. He drew the two rapiers he wore at his hips, holding them at the ready, and gave a mocking laugh.

"Mrowr~! That's quite a punch!"

"He has to actually hit you to do damage, though. Say, are you sure you're okay without backup, Demi-what's-your-name?"

Shiroe heckled, as Demiquas launched a few more fierce punches.

Demiquas's anger seemed to blaze even hotter. "Once I put down this old furry, I'll tear you apart!" he roared.

"Yes, yes. Until then, though, you're fighting me... There is a lady present, and I'd rather not force her to witness anything gruesome. If mew'd like me to hold back, speak up quickly."

"*Shove it!!*"

As Nyanta leapt nimbly out of the way, Demiquas's attacks seemed to completely ignore the distance between them. He launched two or three destructive left hooks from a stance like a shot-putter's. Nyanta deflected some of the attacks with his rapiers, but several hit home with heavy thuds.

In the first place, Demiquas had nearly half again as much HP as Nyanta. On top of that, even if Nyanta evaded more than half of them, the few jabs and kicks that got through were heavy enough to drain his HP.

"C'mon, *c'mon!*"

Demiquas closed in, his face radiant with fierce joy.

Demiquas was a Monk. Monk was one of the three Warrior classes, along with Guardian and Samurai. All the Warrior classes specialized in drawing enemy attacks on the front line and were designed with an emphasis on Defense. That meant that Monks, who were lightly equipped and couldn't wear anything sturdier than leather armor, were unusual for the category.

In *Elder Tales*, spells and sword techniques were known as "special skills." In addition to proper names and effects, each special skill came with set values for required MP, cast time, and recast time. Cast time was the amount of time between the point when a player selected a special skill and the point when the skill activated—the equivalent of "charge" time. Recast time was the amount of time that had to pass after a special skill was used before it could be used again. During recast time, it was possible to do other things, but one couldn't use the special skill they'd just used. Most powerful skills couldn't be used again right away.

For example, most of the special skills used by the Samurai class had long recast times. This meant that Samurai fought by taking careful aim with special skills that had powerful effects.

In contrast, the recast time for Monks' convenient major special skills was short. Specific examples included the Lightning Straight and Wyvern Kick skills. Monks were excellent at paying out unbroken wave attacks by using many moves with a focus on attacks with high basic performance.

Although their armor was the thinnest of the Warrior classes, Monks were light on their feet, and they had the best evasive abilities of the three. In addition, just as Guardians had special shield-based Defense skills, Monks had several evasive Defense skills, such as Phantom Step, which let the player evade an opponent's attack by leaving a body double in their place, and Dragon Scale Stance, which protected the player from flame and ice attacks. Monks' Defense was supported by the player's physical abilities and special skills, not by their equipment. Monks could acquire first-rate fighting abilities even without rare, high-level gear, and they had a solid reputation for being the handiest of the Warrior classes.

"Whassamatter? Huh? Attack already! Is Defense all you got?!"

Nyanta took two steps back, managing to parry Demiquas's attack. However, Demiquas closed the several meters between them in one move, with a flying kick wrapped in a dark green aura. Nyanta evaded that kick as well, but Demiquas segued into a one-two punch without even blinking.

Demiquas's kick technique was a Wyvern Kick. The skill had forward-thrusting collision detection, and Demiquas activated it in order to close distances. Since he was using it as a move technique to check Nyanta and close the gap between them, he always got in close to Nyanta and paid out a rapid serial left-and-right attack, which meant that Nyanta couldn't keep his distance.

He's pretty good. He isn't giving Nyanta any room to run.

Shiroe was secretly impressed. Relief was spreading among the

Briganteers, whose unstable atmosphere had betrayed the guild's internal conflicts up until a few moments ago. It was the reaction of men who were confident that their leader's complete victory was assured.

However, as Nyanta parried a wide hook, he lightly jabbed a knee into Demiquas's vulnerable side from point-blank range, then used that graceful attack as a foothold from which to change his stance in midair.

"Mrowr. Meowr!"

With a rapier attack that seemed to split the air, Nyanta slashed through the guard on Demiquas's thigh, leaving a wound as if the Monk had been jabbed with an ice pick. Shifting his grip and taking a new defensive stance, Nyanta watched Demiquas with steely eyes, letting the tips of his rapiers skim through the air like swallows.

Nyanta was a Swashbuckler. It was one of the close-range attack classes, and one of the few that fought with two swords. It was characterized by lightning-fast serial attacks that made the best of the weapons in both hands and by wide-range attacks that made use of rotation. Taken singly, Swashbuckler attacks had less force than an Assassin's, but they were speed fighters that accumulated overall damage through multiple attacks.

As a class, Swashbucklers were capable of a wide range of variations, depending on the Swashbuckler's choice of weapons and the special skills they decided to focus on. Nyanta's fighting style featured twin rapiers. The attack speed of this style was second only to the twin daggers style—where the player held a knife in each hand—and it made its user one of the fastest fighters around.

Another feature that distinguished the Swashbuckler class was their various sword attacks with bonus effects. The Swashbucklers' exquisitely accurate attacks used Attack Speed Reduction, Evasion Performance Reduction, Defense Reduction, and other effects to steal the targets' strengths and expose their shortcomings as even more fatal weaknesses.

"Your hairy thighs are on display. Just look at all that fuzz. Mew could practically braid it."

Nyanta teased. Demiquas's face went purple. However, Nyanta

didn't let the opening escape him. His rapiers accurately punctured holes in all four of Demiquas's limbs with a light noise—almost like the click of typewriter keys—that didn't seem as if it could be coming from a weapon.

The four wounds left in the Monk's arms were known as Viper Slash. By wounding the tendons in the player's arm, the attack lowered the hit rate of their attacks for several dozen seconds. The three wounds in his thigh were Bloody Piercing. By cutting the legs, the attack reduced the player's agility and lowered their evasive capabilities. Nyanta was working to strip away his opponent's fighting power with a surgeon's eye and the will to decisively execute his plan. The calm adviser who'd been dubbed "the Retiree" was nowhere to be seen.

"Gwah! Quit jumping around, freak! Fight fair and square!"

"Coming from mew, 'fair and square' sounds polluted."

In terms of HP, Demiquas had the advantage. Nyanta's HP had already been drained to 30 percent. As expected of a Warrior class, Demiquas still had more than twice Nyanta's HP left. Right now, though, anyone on the battlefield could see that the lone, lanky Swashbuckler held the initiative. Thrust and stab, flick and dazzle—slim steel lines even thinner than a fingertip drew a lacy filigree of silver and sparks in the air, forming an ironclad defense that thwarted Demiquas. The speed and attack powers Demiquas had at the beginning of the battle were long gone. Most importantly, his HP and MP were draining away along with the blood he was losing, moment by moment, from his pierced limbs.

The Briganteers, who had been reassured by Demiquas's activity just moments before, suddenly began to mutter among themselves. The mutter held the fear and unease that their leader might actually lose, coupled with irrepressible curiosity and a furtive joy. In all likelihood, Demiquas was a tyrant within his guild as well. The Briganteers seemed to feel an ill-natured, detached glee at the idea that he might lose in public.

Shiroe picked up on that emotion. He signaled to Serara.

Serara, who'd been watching Nyanta's gallant fight so desperately that she didn't even notice her fingernails biting into her palms, came back to herself with a jolt when Shiroe touched her shoulder. The voice in her ear, so faint she could barely hear it, said, "At my signal, cast a Pulse Recovery spell on all parties."

Serara's eyes widened. Of course, as a healer—even a very minor one—she fully intended to recover Nyanta once he won, but why "at my signal"? ...And why not just Nyanta, but everybody? She was about to ask Shiroe when she heard an unbelievable yell.

"Dammit! You cocky little— Enough of your lousy duel!! Healer! Recover these wounds in my arms and legs! Assassin squad! Skin this cat bastard!!"

Demiquas, finally unable to take the brilliance of the swordsman's techniques, ordered the Briganteers to attack en masse.

▶ **6**

That angry roar caused a momentary split on the battlefield.

The Briganteers had traded non-player characters as slaves. They'd threatened and killed players and done even worse, and precisely *because* they had, for an instant, that order made them hesitate.

The Briganteers were a band of outlaws. However, in a true state of lawlessness, outlaws could never form a group. Complete anarchy made it impossible for communities to exist for any length of time. Outlaws had their own particular brand of order, and in extreme terms, that order was power. Violence.

The Briganteers, a band of outlaws, were ruled by power. Their leader Demiquas had had his vaunted attack power sealed, was losing his ability to evade, and was being carved up by rapiers—a weapon he normally scorned as being "for women and children"—in a one-on-one duel. In response to the reality that he was, in fact, being carved up, he had ordered them to surround and destroy the enemy with a roar that was—no matter how you looked at it—an SOS.

"Is it really okay to follow orders from a leader like this? If we obey him, will we turn into losers someday, too?" That idea made even the outlaw Briganteers hesitate.

Let them hesitate, get nervous, jump at shadows, and freeze up. If they do, we luck out.

...But the hesitation lasted only an instant.

True, their leader was a sorry sight, but even a violent band of out-laws had a reputation to uphold. As a matter of fact, being a band of outlaws made their reputation *more* important to them, not less. A big part of the reason the Briganteers had been able to do what-ever they wanted in Susukino even as they exploited other players was that the guild had a reputation as an invincible gang of thugs. Unless they maintained their reign of terror by any means necessary, they'd become the hunted. This terror, peculiar to habitual hunters, decided the group's course of action in just three seconds. Their goal was less to save their leader than to silence the three players who'd witnessed this debacle. Once that decision was made, the outlaws descended like an avalanche, war cries in every throat, hell-bent on engulfing Nyanta.

However, not one member of Shiroe's group had wasted those three seconds. The approaching wave of eight bellowing Brigan-teers was blocked by Naotsugu, who'd appeared like a gust of wind. Rather than slam on the brakes at this sudden appearance from out-side their field of vision, the Briganteers bore down with even greater malice.

"Anchor Howl!!"

Naotsugu yelled. It was a special skill for Guardians, the fortresses of the front line, which drew all enemies within range to them. The eight Briganteers stopped in front of Naotsugu as if they'd been nailed in place.

"Nyanta!! They're going to—!!"

"Begin recovery!"

"Y-yes, sir! Pulse Recovery!!"

At Shiroe's command, Serara began to chant the most powerful recovery spell she had.

Pulse Recovery was a special recovery skill unique to Druids. It was roughly equivalent to the Kannagis' Damage Block and the Clerics' Response Activated Recovery. In simple terms, Pulse Recovery was a spell for continuous HP recovery. It was settable, and for between ten and thirty seconds, each companion targeted by the spell would recover a certain amount of HP per second. Although it didn't recover as much per second as a normal recovery spell, the total was far superior, and the spell's MP efficiency was also excellent.

In addition, Pulse Recovery had one advantage even greater than its high efficiency: Once set, the caster was free to do other things. The player could use that free time to attack, defend, or do anything else necessary.

However—

"It won't work! I can't keep it up! My level isn't high enough!"

Serara cried miserably.

In *Elder Tales*, healers' abilities were key. Working in combination, a trained healer and vanguard warrior could cancel out the damage inflicted by four enemies on their level.

That said, Serara was currently level 19. At level 90, Naotsugu's Defense was off the charts, but he'd never be able to withstand physical attacks from the eight Briganteers, whose levels were also high.

"Ignore Naotsugu for now. Concentrate on recovering Nyanta. Calm down and watch our allies' HP. Don't worry about doing the impossible. Just stay focused on what you can do."

Shiroe spoke to Serara, his voice calm. She was very near to panicking.

His words were stronger than she'd expected, and Serara felt her strength return as though she'd been smacked on the back. What the healing classes could do was heal, Shiroe told her.

Meanwhile, on the other front line, away from Naotsugu, Nyanta and Demiquas's battle was nearing its climax. Demiquas seemed to have received a recovery spell from the rear: The wounds in his arms had healed, and his attack power was back. Although the wounds in his legs were still there, he'd probably decided to forget evading and fight. Demiquas's face was much calmer.

To begin with, Demiquas was a Monk, one of the Warrior classes. Even though Swashbucklers were a direct attack class, they were one of the Weapon Attack classes, and their fundamental Health was different. If Demiquas was able to get help from his rear guard, he was sure he could bully his way through on Health, even if the battle degenerated into a messy brawl. The Druid chit seemed to be healing the swordsman he was facing, but there was no way the total amount could surpass the damage he inflicted. Full of confidence, Demiquas raged.

"C'mon! C'mon, *c'mon*! What are those swords of yours, toys?! You think a flimsy punk like you can protect anybody?!"

"I beg your pardon. Rapiers are a gentleman's weapon."

"I'm gonna shut that smart mouth of yours! Look, your Warrior buddy's going down!"

"I wouldn't be so sure."

Nyanta and Demiquas's battle grew even fiercer as they traded swords and fists, silver light and dull blows.

Enveloped in a thick cloud of dust, Naotsugu really had been driven into a corner. The continuous wave of attacks from his eight opponents had cut his HP down to 2,400. He'd lost a full 80 percent. However, even under the circumstances, Naotsugu kept his cool, maintaining his narrow stance, fielding the Briganteers' attacks, and controlling their formation.

Staying calm, even in a situation where panic was likely, was an essential ability for a first class vanguard. However, to Serara, who was short on experience, Naotsugu's almost eerily smooth movements seemed filled with awe-inspiring energy.

"Prepare to cast."

Shiroe's voice was a whisper. With the sound of her own heart galloping loudly in her ears, Serara answered, "O-okay!" Her voice had gone shrill and nervous.

"I'm going for it, Shiroe! Castle of Stone!!"

As Naotsugu yelled, he pulled his shield in and took a solid stance. His shield, his armor, and even his sword took on the ageless sheen of marble, scattering magical power and energy.

"Wha... What the heck?!"

"Ignore it, he's almost down. Finish him!!"

"Take that! Assassinate!!"

Apparently one of the eight Briganteers was an Assassin. He launched a lethal attack meant to inflict massive damage. With an air-scorching, grating sound, his sword sank through Naotsugu's armor, delivering a fatal blow.

...Or that's what should have happened. Instead, the Assassin's attack bounced off Naotsugu's shield with a clang.

Castle of Stone was one of the Guardians' powerful defensive techniques. It was an emergency move, and it only lasted for ten seconds, but during that time, no attack could damage the player. Naotsugu, now a marble fortress, held the front line with an unbreakable shield.

"What did I tell mew? Naotsugucchi isn't that easy."

"Now, Serara! Cast a layered recovery on Naotsugu!!"

Serara took a hasty step forward, stretching her hands up toward the sky. She chanted a Pulse Recovery spell meant for individuals, layering it over the Pulse Recovery spell that was already in effect for all players, and she didn't stop there. On top of the two layered set spells, she began to chant an instant recovery spell. Using every last drop of her limited level-19 power, she continued sending all the recovery spells she knew to the front line.

As a healer, there was just one thing she could do: Use her recovery spells to protect the players who were protecting her. The familiar voice of her guild master, a Cleric, echoed in her ears.

The true benefit of Pulse Recovery lay in the fact that once it was set the caster could use the remaining time to chant additional recovery spells. The potential of a Druid who concentrated everything they had on recovery was unimaginably high. The class's instantaneous recovery power easily surpassed that of the other two healing classes. Even if the caster was level 19, this wasn't a force to be taken lightly. Under Serara's rapid succession of spells, Naotsugu's HP, which had already fallen below 20 percent, recovered before their very eyes.

"Stalling for time isn't gonna save you!" Meanwhile, as he closed in on Nyanta, Demiquas's rage was growing. Castle of Stone certainly was a powerful defensive technique. As a Monk, another Warrior class, the technique was tough enough to make him jealous. However, even the most powerful techniques had weaknesses. In Castle of Stone's case, it was the length of its recast time. The unbreakable technique could only be used once every ten minutes.

In ten minutes, he could kill the players in front of him twenty times over. In any case, the fact that the Warrior had used Castle of Stone at all obviously meant he wasn't able to stand up to the Briganteers' collective attack. The technique could only shut out ten seconds' worth of physical damage in ten minutes. Ten seconds out of six hundred. Put that way, Castle of Stone wasn't an invincible secret technique. It was clearly a last resort.

When Castle of Stone's effect wore off, these guys would be history. To Demiquas, that future was already a fact. His keen attacks were rapidly driving Nyanta into a corner. As Serara kept an eye on her allies' statuses, she couldn't help lamenting her weakness.

The Guardian who was fielding eight Briganteers on the front line, and Nyanta, who'd chivalrously shielded her all this time, were getting hurt. Even if she poured all her strength into recovery, she couldn't save the two of them, and the MP she needed for the spells were draining away rapidly as she pushed the limits of her power.

"I'd like to go soon, Shiroechi."

"Anytime you're ready, Captain Nyanta."

However, quite apart from Serara's anguish, Shiroe and Nyanta's exchange was as cheerful as a clear blue sky.

In a movement as smooth as a willow in the wind, Nyanta stepped right into Demiquas's chest. Although he was momentarily startled, Demiquas raised his knee in a kick intended to send the thin swordsman flying. However, in the next instant, Nyanta had launched himself into the air, using Demiquas's raised knee as a foothold.

Silver light flashed.

The rapiers Nyanta held in both hands sliced the wind, dancing with the speed of indigo lightning. Three, four, five— That was as far as Serara managed to follow. Nyanta's swords, which seemed to have generated countless copies of themselves, slashed with pinpoint accuracy through the bright blue brambles that had abruptly appeared all over Demiquas's body.

Swashbuckler attacks were the fastest of all twelve classes. Nyanta's multistage two-bladed attack was further sharpened by Shiroe's attack ability reinforcement, and on top of that, he kept triggering the Sewn-Bind Hostage trap that Shiroe had set.

Nyanta's swords.

Shiroe's Sewn-Bind Hostage.

In less than two seconds, the double-layered attack was executed ten times. With each slash from Nyanta, the activated spell burst like a flashbulb, sending a shock wave across the area. Just as the explosion that occurs in the tight chamber of a gun magazine is made more destructive by its compression. Demiquas, who had frozen in his tracks, staggered as if he were being shoved from all sides by invisible enemies and expired before he had time to utter a word.

"Wha—?!"

"The guild master just—"

Confusion spread rapidly.

A level-90 Warrior with a healer supporting him had dropped like a stone in the blink of an eye. The more experience the players had with *Elder Tales*, the greater the superstition and despair the sight instilled.

"Nyanta…"

The emotion was echoed in Serara's dazed murmur. She couldn't understand the lightning-fast battle she'd just seen unfold.

"Drop your swords, people!"

Naotsugu yelled. The Briganteers looked at each other, then went pale as a scream rang out behind them.

At its source, they saw their fallen healer and the guild's second-in-command, the gray-robed Rondarg, cowering, one of his arms severed. The black-haired girl—the player who'd made the most efficient use of that empty three seconds—had sheathed her delicate form in the merciless aura of a lethal weapon, and her short sword was pressed to Rondarg's neck.

▶ 7

Akatsuki, who had seen exactly what Serara saw, did have a fairly good idea of what had happened. Adventurer bodies were high performance, and apparently that performance wasn't limited to agility and physical strength: Their kinetic vision was also better than it had been in their old world.

Akatsuki had studied kendo since she was small, but she was absolutely sure she wouldn't have been able to follow the speed of those swords in the real world. Even here, she'd only been able to follow half of the maneuver at best. It would be more accurate to say that she'd "seen" it by mentally piecing together the multiple fragments of visual information she'd managed to pick up and revising them through deduction.

Akatsuki was an Assassin, the Weapon Attack class with the highest attack power, and even her ultimate attack wouldn't have been able to take out a level-90 Monk. Of course, Akatsuki had neutralized the healer who'd been supporting Demiquas, and his HP probably hadn't been fully charged. Even so, it should have been impossible to defeat a Warrior that quickly.

Battles in *Elder Tales* tended to be battles of attrition. In this world, "certain-kill moves" were only a figure of speech and were almost never literally lethal. In a fight between players of the same level, even the strongest player would have to pay out several dozen attacks in order to win. If healers were standing by, battles could go on indefinitely, and it was rare for there to be a victory at all. The more experience a player had in *Elder Tales*, the better they understood that fact. Where the game was concerned, it was just common sense.

The secret behind the freakish damage Nyanta had inflicted was probably the shining blue brambles. Shiroe's Sewn-Bind Hostage was a settable trap spell used by Enchanters. The spell set five briers on a target's body, and each brier worked with an ally's attack to inflict about one thousand in damage. However, even if all the briers were triggered, it would only inflict five thousand in damage. That would have been a bit more than a third of Demiquas's HP. Even with the damage from Nyanta's attacks added in, it wouldn't have been enough to defeat him.

In all the group training they'd done together, Akatsuki had become very well acquainted with the spells Shiroe used most. Sewn-Bind Hostage was one of Shiroe's best spells, and Akatsuki recognized it just by seeing those bramble-like effects. The spell's recast time was fifteen seconds.

In all likelihood, after Shiroe set the trap on Demiquas, Nyanta had waited fourteen seconds.

He'd parried Demiquas's attacks, holding out for those fourteen seconds. During that time, he'd gotten in close and secured a positional advantage, waiting until the time was right. Then, at the appointed instant, he'd leapt into the air and paid out a series of five attacks with his left rapier. The attacks had pierced the brambles as if drawn directly to them, triggering the additional damage. In that instant, the recast time had ended, and Shiroe had hit Demiquas with another Sewn-Bind Hostage. Nyanta, still airborne, had executed a half-turn and paid out another five attacks with his right rapier.

A series of ten attacks from both sides. Two linked Sewn-Bind Hostage spells cast with a pitch-perfect grasp of the recast time. Each of the ten attacks had acted as a trigger, detonating all ten briers.

That was the truth of what Akatsuki had "seen."

However, she'd only managed to see it because she was familiar with the characteristics of that spell from working with Shiroe. There had been no interruption in the airborne Swashbuckler's attacks. Executing ten thrusts in a mere two seconds had to be a special technique peculiar to Swashbucklers.

Ten attacks in two seconds. In simple terms, each attack had taken a fifth of a second. Setting a new Sewn-Bind Hostage in the practically nonexistent pause between the fifth and sixth attacks seemed humanly impossible. The move had been brilliant.

True, with an attack like that one, it would be possible to completely drain a Warrior's HP in an instant, but would it be easy to execute? The answer was an emphatic "no." Akatsuki came very near to biting her lip; she hastily composed her expression. The battle wasn't over yet.

She could feel what she'd seen colliding with what she knew to be common sense.

She'd trained with Shiroe for more than ten days, and she didn't think even she'd be able to copy that maneuver. Those two had pulled off that intricate team play even though they hadn't spoken in ages and didn't seem to have planned it in detail.

From the Briganteers' faces, the shock Akatsuki felt had hit them with a dozen times more force.

Who were these men?

Where had they gotten enough attack power to bury Demiquas?

Could they possibly have leveled up past level 90?

Were they actually a cleanup squad from another district?

That attack, which even Akatsuki hadn't been able to understand without the help of several deductions, would have been impossible to evade by sight. Not only could they not evade it, they couldn't even understand it.

"When did they... That can't be..."

Demiquas had held his guild together with fighting ability that verged on brutality, and although the two hadn't gotten along, Rondarg had supported the Briganteers with his resourcefulness. With both their leaders gone, even though the bandits still had most of their strength left, their will to fight had been completely broken.

"We came through the Depths of Palm,"

Shiroe stepped toward Rondarg, approaching Akatsuki and the captive magic user.

"The distance between Susukino and Akiba isn't so great it can't be crossed. We have the method and the map, and we've called in the information. This party is over."

The facts weren't really so optimistic.

Akatsuki and the others had come this far with the aid of their griffins. Not all players would be able to travel so quickly. The journey up to the Ezzo Empire was still a very long and massive undertaking.

However, Shiroe had probably phrased it categorically on purpose to fan a sense of defeat in the Briganteers. Akatsuki let the short sword she held against Rondarg's neck slip a little, using the cold blade to drive home Shiroe's point.

"We win this battle. We'll be taking your other leader's head with us."

Shiroe quickly took a dagger from his inner pocket and used it to sever Demiquas's head. Akatsuki saw Shiroe's expression cloud slightly at the wet sound of splitting flesh that the dagger made as he brought it down.

...Well, of course. Even if it wouldn't actually kill the player, beheading someone wasn't something any of them wanted to do. However, Shiroe managed to keep his tone callous. There was no telling how much meaning there was in taking someone's head in a world where death didn't exist, but Akatsuki thought it was a price the men should pay. They'd bet themselves in this fight, and they'd lost.

Faced with Shiroe's cold attitude and piercing stare, the Briganteers edged back.

The frozen silence was broken by a griffin's sharp cry. Three griffins appeared from the western sky, flying in a V-shaped formation, and landed rather roughly in front of Shiroe's group.

"Serara, over here!"

Nyanta had sheathed his rapiers, and holding out a hand to Serara, he pulled her in, picked her up bodily, and leapt onto the nearest griffin. Naotsugu, who'd mounted his griffin even more quickly, took a step forward as if to shield Akatsuki. Akatsuki swung her short sword, shaking off the blood. Shiroe stood just beyond her, watching her with the usual look in his eyes: a bit sullen, yet somehow worried.

"Akatsuki, let's go!"

Akatsuki nodded as she'd done many times before. The gesture was filled with the gratitude and respect she couldn't express aloud.

"Let's move! Heading out! Escape city!"

Naotsugu yelled, as if he were declaring a cavalry charge, and his griffin leapt for the sky. Nyanta's sand-colored griffin launched itself after it.

Akatsuki leapt up behind Shiroe, barely touching the fingers of the hand he held out for her. With her reinforced Adventurer's abilities, she could have mounted the griffin without Shiroe's help. However, it was his griffin. Jumping up without a word would have seemed rude, but asking for permission would have felt awkward and artificially distant, so Akatsuki always let Shiroe's hand guide her to her seat.

Shiroe had kept his gaze on the Briganteers right up until the end, but he finally sighed, as if giving up, and spoke to Akatsuki.

"Let's go."

Akatsuki gave a small nod. At the pressure from Shiroe's bootheels, the griffin soared up the slope of the wind, over the dazed, upturned faces of the Briganteers and the heads of the Adventurers who'd come out from Susukino. The three enormous creatures flew away, leaving the echoes of savage, magnificent wingbeats behind them.

Up here, racing through the wind on the back of a griffin, she felt the faint ache from Shiroe and Nyanta's teamwork and the irritation she'd experienced in Susukino scatter into the clear blue sky.

They'd successfully rescued Serara of the Crescent Moon League. They had another week of travel ahead of them before they reached Akiba, but their mission was complete. They'd done it.

The cold wind buffeted Akatsuki, but it couldn't shake her sense of peace. She held tight to Shiroe's back, feeling a quiet satisfaction at having accomplished their mission.

"My liege."

"What, Akatsuki?"

"…Never mind."

"Mm… Let's go home. Back to Akiba."

"Mm-hm."

The wind snatched the words away the moment she spoke them, and the blue air streamed around her and away.

Like larks released from their cages, the three griffins flew, bound for southern skies.

<Log Horizon, Volume 1: The Beginning of Another World—The End>

<ELDER TALES CLASS TABLE>

▶ MAIN CLASSES

[WARRIOR CLASSES]

GUARDIAN
BOASTS THE HIGHEST DEFENSE. ABLE TO ATTRACT ENEMIES WITH TAUNTS.

SAMURAI
USES JAPANESE EQUIPMENT AND TECHNIQUES WITH POWERFUL EFFECTS.

MONK
A BALANCED TYPE. SHORT ON WEAPONRY, BUT HAS FANTASTIC EVASIVE SKILLS.

[WEAPON ATTACK CLASSES]

ASSASSIN
A FOCUSED ATTACKER. SKILLED WITH A WIDE VARIETY OF WEAPONS.

SWASHBUCKLER
A VERSATILE, MOBILE FIGHTER. USES TWO SWORDS.

BARD
A LIGHTLY EQUIPPED WARRIOR. USES A WIDE RANGE OF "SONGS" WITH MAGICAL EFFECTS.

▶ SUBCLASSES *LIST NOT EXHAUSTIVE.

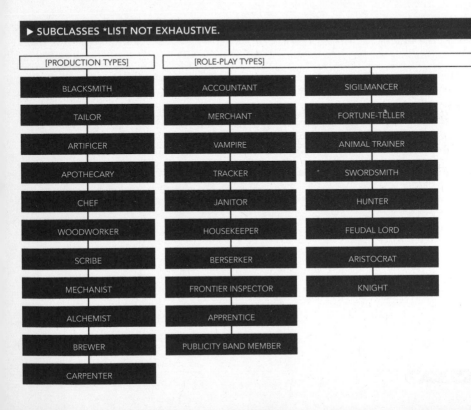

[PRODUCTION TYPES]	[ROLE-PLAY TYPES]	
BLACKSMITH	ACCOUNTANT	SIGILMANCER
TAILOR	MERCHANT	FORTUNE-TELLER
ARTIFICER	VAMPIRE	ANIMAL TRAINER
APOTHECARY	TRACKER	SWORDSMITH
CHEF	JANITOR	HUNTER
WOODWORKER	HOUSEKEEPER	FEUDAL LORD
SCRIBE	BERSERKER	ARISTOCRAT
MECHANIST	FRONTIER INSPECTOR	KNIGHT
ALCHEMIST	APPRENTICE	
BREWER	PUBLICITY BAND MEMBER	
CARPENTER		

[RECOVERY CLASSES]

CLERIC
THE ULTIMATE HEALER. HAS THE GREATEST RECOVERY ABILITIES.

DRUID
A MAGICAL RECOVERY CLASS ALLIED WITH NATURE AND THE SPIRITS.

KANNAGI
A PREVENTATIVE RECOVERY CLASS THAT BLOCKS DAMAGE.

[MAGIC ATTACK CLASSES]

SORCERER
SPECIALIZES IN DIRECTLY INFLICTING DAMAGE ON OPPONENTS.

SUMMONER
SPECIALIZES IN SUMMONING AND CONTROLLING MYTHICAL BEASTS AND SPIRITS.

ENCHANTER
SPECIALIZES IN MANAGING ABNORMAL STATUSES AND MP.

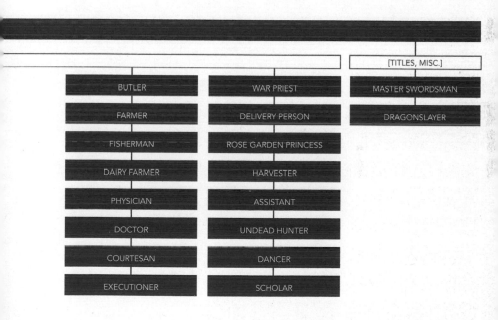

		[TITLES, MISC.]
BUTLER	WAR PRIEST	MASTER SWORDSMAN
FARMER	DELIVERY PERSON	DRAGONSLAYER
FISHERMAN	ROSE GARDEN PRINCESS	
DAIRY FARMER	HARVESTER	
PHYSICIAN	ASSISTANT	
DOCTOR	UNDEAD HUNTER	
COURTESAN	DANCER	
EXECUTIONER	SCHOLAR	

AFTERWORD

To my first-time readers, it's great to meet you!

To those of you who know me from the Internet, it's great to see you again!

This is Mamare Touno.

Thank you very much for buying *Log Horizon, Vol. 1: The Beginning of Another World*. This book is an edited and revised version of an online serial I started writing in April 2010. When the story was turned into a book, I changed the setting a bit and revised the text to improve the quality of the writing and its readability. I'll be thrilled if you add it to your personal collections.

...Enough of the boring preamble. I think I'll talk about Little Sister Touno. Yes, the rumors are true: I have a little sister, and she has a distressingly weak constitution. I'm a fairly dim bulb myself, but Sister Touno is a very silly creature indeed.

A long time ago, when we were little, I told her that all the eggs in *komochi-shishamo* (Japanese smelt with intact roe) were injected in through the fishes' butts with a syringe, and she believed me. Even now, I remember her nodding earnestly as I told her, "Workers in Sakhalin toil away with their syringes in a huge, freezing cold factory."

The other day, she'd completely forgotten I was the one who'd introduced her to the *Shishamo* Injector Theory, and she let it drop in conversation as trivia.

Well, yes, it's trivia, but it's *fake* trivia.

Of course, I didn't call her on it. I just looked very serious and acted impressed, but apparently she finally found out the truth from somebody else, and she got really mad at me.

So, Sister Touno is another few steps up the stairway to adulthood. Still, since the stairway she's climbing is a lot like the down escalator, it's hard to tell whether she's actually going up or whether the scenery's just scrolling backward.

Later, when I ran an Internet search on the *Shishamo* Injector Theory, I discovered that it's actually a rumor with a bit more truth behind it than your average urban legend. Real life trumps my ability to fib on demand.

When I told Sister Touno, "Apparently they do sometimes inject eggs into male *shishamo* and sell them," she pulled the futon over her head and refused to talk to me. I don't think she's going to believe anything I tell her about this anymore. It takes a long time to build up trust and only an instant to lose it. —Although, in this case, I still think she's a dim bulb for letting me fool her for almost a decade.

That said, my memory has never been the greatest, and neither has Sister Touno's. After a while, I'm pretty sure her head will fill up with thoughts about dinner, and she'll completely forget.

As you can see, Sister Touno and I are as chummy as England and Ireland, so I told her, "Hey, remember that story I told you? You know, *Log Horizon.* —Get this: It's going to be in bookstores," but she didn't believe me at all. She said, "Quit lying, stupid big brother," or something like that.

That's only to be expected. Even I still don't quite believe the publishing thing. Sister Touno may think everything I say is a lie, but letting her think that is fun, too, so I haven't tried to make her understand.

…So that's what *Log Horizon* went through before ending up in your hands. The characters kick up more of a ruckus than they did in the online version, and I think they'll drive the story. The character status screens at the beginning of each chapter symbolize this. As a matter of fact, the items listed on each of these screens were submitted by readers via Twitter in January 2011. There were close to three hundred items submitted, and the items I used came from IGM_masamune, LAN, akinon29, ebius1, gontan_, izumino, kane_yon, oddmake, roki_a, sawame_ja, and vaiso. Thank you so much!! I can't give your names here, but I'm grateful to everyone who submitted suggestions. Shiroe and the other characters are psyched, too.

Log Horizon began online, and I'd like to keep running projects like this one from *Volume 2* onward. For details and the latest news, check out http://mamare.net. The site has all sorts of other non–*Log Horizon* Mamare Touno information, too.

Finally, I'd like to thank Shoji Masuda, who produced this book; Kazuhiro Hara, who drew supremely cool illustrations for it; Tsuba-kiya Design, the agency who designed it; Oha, who proofread it; and F——ta of the Enterbrain editorial department! Thank you very much!

If you read this book and enjoy Shiroe and the other characters' journey, then the book will truly be complete. Bon appétit.

Mamare "I love shishamo*" Touno*

▶LOG HORIZON, VOLUME 1
MAMARE TOUNO
ILLUSTRATION BY KAZUHIRO HARA

▶TRANSLATION BY TAYLOR ENGEL

▶AUTHOR: **MAMARE TOUNO**

▶LOG HORIZON, VOLUME 1:
THE BEGINNING OF ANOTHER WORLD

▶FIRST PUBLISHED IN JAPAN IN 2011 BY
KADOKAWA CORPORATION ENTERBRAIN.
ENGLISH TRANSLATION RIGHTS ARRANGED
WITH KADOKAWA CORPORATION ENTERBRAIN,
THROUGH TUTTLE-MORI AGENCY, INC., TOKYO.

▶SUPERVISION: **SHOJI MASUDA**

▶ILLUSTRATION: **KAZUHIRO HARA**

▶YEN ON
1290 AVENUE OF THE AMERICAS
NEW YORK, NY 10104
WWW.YENPRESS.COM

▶YEN ON IS AN IMPRINT OF
YEN PRESS, LLC.

▶THE YEN ON NAME AND LOGO ARE
TRADEMARKS OF YEN PRESS, LLC.

▶FIRST YEN ON EDITION: APRIL 2015

▶ISBN: 978-0-316-38305-9

10 9 8 7 6

▶LSC-C

▶PRINTED IN THE UNITED STATES OF AMERICA

▶AUTHOR: MAMARE TOUNO

A STRANGE LIFE-FORM THAT INHABITS THE TOKYO BOKUTOU SHITAMACHI AREA. IT'S BEEN TOSSING HALF-BAKED TEXT INTO A CORNER OF THE INTERNET SINCE THE YEAR 2000 OR SO. IT'S A FULLY AUTOMATIC, TEXT-LOVING MACRO THAT EATS AND DISCHARGES TEXT. IT DEBUTED AT THE END OF 2010 WITH *MAOYUU: MAOU YUUSHA* (*MAOYUU: DEMON KING AND HERO*). *LOG HORIZON* IS A RESTRUCTURED VERSION OF A NOVEL THAT RAN ON THE WEBSITE *SHOUSETSUKA NI NAROU* (*SO YOU WANT TO BE A NOVELIST*).

WEBSITE: HTTP://WWW.MAMARE.NET

▶SUPERVISION: SHOJI MASUDA

AS A GAME DESIGNER, HE'S WORKED ON *RINDA KYUUBU* (*RINDA CUBE*) AND *ORE NO SHIKABANE WO KOETE YUKE* (*STEP OVER MY DEAD BODY*), AMONG OTHERS. ALSO ACTIVE AS A NOVELIST, HE'S RELEASED THE *ONIGIRI NUEKO* (*ONI KILLER NUEKO*) SERIES, THE *HARUKA* SERIES, *JOHN & MARY: FUTARI HA SHOUKIN KASEGI* (*JOHN & MARY: BOUNTY HUNTERS*), *KIZUDARAKE NO BIINA* (*BEENA, COVERED IN WOUNDS*), AND MORE. HIS LATEST EFFORT IS HIS FIRST CHILDREN'S BOOK, *TOUMEI NO NEKO TO TOSHI UE NO IMOUTO* (*THE TRANSPARENT CAT AND THE OLDER LITTLE SISTER*). HE HAS ALSO WRITTEN *GEEMU DEZAIN NOU MASUDA SHINJI NO HASSOU TO WAZA* (*GAME DESIGN BRAIN: SHINJI MASUDA'S IDEAS AND TECHNIQUES*).

TWITTER ACCOUNT: SHOJIMASUDA

▶ILLUSTRATION: KAZUHIRO HARA

AN ILLUSTRATOR WHO LIVES IN ZUSHI. ORIGINALLY A HOME GAME DEVELOPER. IN ADDITION TO ILLUSTRATING BOOKS, HE'S ALSO ACTIVE IN MANGA AND DESIGN. LATELY, HE'S BEEN HAVING FUN FLYING A BIOKITE WHEN HE GOES ON WALKS.

WEBSITE: HTTP://WWW.NINEFIVE95.COM/IG/

Adventurer, you whose weight is borne by your winged soul! The mystical world of Theldesia is home to dragons and giants, magical beasts, and demihumans. Fragrant green winds blow across this new yet ancient land that opens before you like a blank page. Fill it with your life.